CALCULATED RISK

CALCULATED RISK

P.I.V.O.T. LAB CHRONICLES™ BOOK TWO

MICHAEL ANDERLE

LMBPN Publishing
PMB 196, 2540 South Maryland Pkwy
Las Vegas, NV 89109

First US Edition, November, 2020
(Previously published as a part of *Too Young To Die*)
eBook ISBN: 978-1-64971-297-4
Print ISBN: 978-1-64971-298-1

THE CALCULATED RISK TEAM

Thanks to the Beta Readers
John Ashmore, Theresa Holmes, Nicole Emens, Larry Omans,
Allen Collins

Thanks to the JIT Readers

Allen Collins
Angel LaVey
Billie Leigh Kellar
Dave Hicks
Deb Mader
Diane L. Smith
Jeff Eaton
Jeff Goode
Kerry Mortimer

If I've missed anyone, please let me know!

Editor
The Skyhunter Editing Team

CHAPTER ONE

"This, above all, is our duty to our constituents." Tad Williams looked out over those gathered there and tried to make eye contact with a few senators in particular. "In this room, most of us have made campaign promises that others would be horrified by." He grinned when there was a laugh. "Maybe your constituents and mine have different opinions on some things. Maybe they have different opinions on most things. And, let's be honest, every one of us here has people who voted against us. So, in every vote, we have to ask ourselves, what is our duty to *everyone* we represent? And the answer is always the same—we do what we believe is right.

"With the greatest of respect to this bill's sponsors, it will harm their constituents and mine. I was elected to represent people, not a party, and that is why I cross the aisle on this bill and vote nay."

A storm of applause from the bill's detractors followed and stony silence from some of the members of his party. Several refused to meet his gaze as he returned to his seat. The energy in the chamber felt almost electric to him.

Of course, that electricity seemed confined to the more junior senators. The senior ones talked quietly to each other and their aides, already focused on the next vote, the next meeting, and the next initiative. One or two had begun to leave the chamber, and a few empty seats told of others who had already gone.

He shook his head as he sat. They'd all been elected to weigh in on matters that affected their constituents, and this bill would affect everyone in the country. No one had any business calling themselves a senator if they chose not to be there for issues like this.

The vote was taken, and Tad was surprised at how steady his hands were when he pressed the button. Two weeks before, his stomach had been in knots and he'd hardly been able to sleep. With his son's life in the balance, the pharmaceutical lobbyists had offered him the answer to all his prayers if he voted aye on this bill.

And blackmail if he didn't.

Several of his fellow senators, as well as news outlets and aides, had asked him what made him stand up to both the lobbyists and his party whip, and he'd answered all of them the same way—that this was what was best for his constituents.

That wasn't the whole truth, though.

The real tipping point had come as he watched Justin fighting for his life. The same companies who lobbied him had blackballed a life-saving treatment years before, one a new company was now trying to revive. The treatment—an immersive alternate reality that worked like a video game—stimulated the brain to heal itself and wake up and after Justin's car accident, that healing was something he desperately needed. It was also something that conventional treatments did not provide.

Tad had never been a fan of video games. He'd wanted to go hunting or fishing with his son. Like most fathers, he'd wanted to throw a football around, which was something Mary made him stop trying after the fifth broken window. When Justin lost himself in a make-believe world full of vampires, dragons, or spaceships, his father wanted to beat his head against a wall.

Then he'd seen Justin play this one.

Despite himself, he recognized much of his younger self in how his son played. There was the desire for acclaim…mostly from beautiful women. There was also the devil-may-care attitude toward risk and the pigheaded insistence on going directly to the most difficult target, strength and aptitude be damned. Tad had gotten more than a few black eyes and bloody noses from that in his teenage years.

What he hadn't expected was the young man's sense of justice. Lurking behind the desire to be the hero was a sense of obligation that extended even to people he knew didn't exist. He had listened to his son's fiery speeches as he exhorted his allies to fight on and villagers to stand up to a tyrant. He'd seen him throw himself into mortal danger to protect those he fought alongside.

Tad had known that when Justin woke up—and he had to wake up because his father could not even contemplate another option—he wanted him to see that he was someone who did the right thing too. He wanted to be someone his son could respect. For years, he'd tried to make his son into someone like him without realizing that Justin was lightyears beyond him in some ways.

The speaker stood and made his way toward the podium, and Tad straightened quickly in anticipation. This was it, the moment when he found out if his speech had made any dent in the balance of votes. His hands clenched as he looked at the board where the split-second ticker of votes showed before the totals populated. Was it enough?

"The nays have it," he heard dimly, and he lowered his head with a laugh that sounded more like a wheeze. Seven of his fellow senators had changed their minds, and although he had no clue if his speech was what had tipped the balance, he knew he had done what was right.

"Senator." A man came to shake his hand. There was a twinkle in his eye—he and Tad had argued opposing sides of several votes before this one, to the point that when one of them stood to talk, everyone looked automatically at the other. This was the first time they'd agreed on a vote, and the other senator clearly found it as amusing as he did. "I assume next week, we'll be back to business as usual?"

"Count on it," Tad told him with a laugh. "I can't wait to see what drivel you come up with on the infrastructure bill."

"With all due respect, Senator, you're confusing my opinions with yours." The other man left with a wide grin and his aides hurried after him with their arms full of folders.

"Senator Williams?" One of his aides tapped him on the shoulder. "Your wife called and said the car is close. Your plane is waiting and we have you on the red-eye back."

"Thanks, Kyle." He handed the man his briefcase. "Text me if anything comes up."

"I will. Also, sir, you should know there are numerous reporters outside and they'll definitely want to talk to you. Verge News had a commentator on this morning saying you'd never vote nay."

"Next time, maybe they'll listen to what I say," he responded. He followed the rush of people into the atrium and pushed toward the door. "Is there any spinach in my teeth? Wine on my tie?"

"What do you eat for breakfast?" Kyle asked rhetorically. "And no, sir, you're good."

"Excellent, thank you." Tad took a breath and exhaled quickly before he stepped out into the crush of reporters, and—exactly as Kyle had predicted—several shouted his name. "Hello. What can I do for you?"

"Senator Williams," one called, "can you discuss why you made a deal with Senator Horitz on this bill?"

"Senator Horitz and I did not make a deal," he said patiently. "Both of us happen to believe this bill is not in the interests of our constituents. Believe me, we were as surprised as everyone else to discover we'd agreed on something." A round of laughter drew a smile from him. He was tired but he genuinely enjoyed this part. He liked to imagine that his constituents saw each word he said as well as the larger meaning behind them—*I'm doing what you voted me in to do. I've got your back.*

"Senator Williams." A woman raised her hand. "Is it true that you've had your son, Justin, transferred to an unlicensed facility for a non-FDA-approved treatment?"

A sudden silence settled over the group around Tad. Nearby, reporters continued to shout to get the attention of other senators, but all of those around him were as blindsided as he was. All he could see right now was the woman's careful, reporter-esque smile.

He had no idea what he would say to that question, but rage and panic had begun to build in his chest in equal measure. A hand slid into his and he jumped, but Mary smiled calmly at him. She offered no word of explanation as she led him away, and the reporters parted silently to let him through.

"Did you hear?" Tad asked numbly.

"Yes." She was still smiling but he knew this particular smile. It was the one she'd worn at family Christmases more than once when she was furious with someone but far too polite to show it. She nodded a thank you to the agent who held the car door open for her and looked at Tad as he folded himself in beside her. Still wearing her pretend smile, she waited until the car lurched into motion before she shook her head. "They shouldn't be allowed to bring children into it."

"I'll sponsor a bill," he said but the automatic joke emerged from his mouth with far too much bitterness. "Jesus Christ."

"Tad."

"Sorry." He gave her a tired smile.

"Well, now I know where Justin got it." She rapped his knuckles affectionately.

"Justin has far outstripped me in the inventiveness of his expletives." He began to relax as the crowd grew farther away, but anger and exhaustion crept in to replace the tension. "So, this is what Metcalfe is doing. He must have decided an affair wasn't newsworthy enough so he's having the press twist what's going on with Justin…if that even was the press."

"I have no doubt." Mary shook her head. "There's always a news outlet looking to break the newest story, whether or not there's a shred of evidence behind it."

"That's what worries me." He leaned his head back. "There is evidence. It doesn't mean what they say it does, but it's there. And with this…who knows how they'll twist it?"

"Son of a…what psychopath arranged these cords?" Jacob crouched and peered at the underside of the desk.

"That would be you," Nick commented from above. "As I recall, your exact verbage was, 'I don't fucking care how they're fucking arranged, I just fucking want to know if it fucking works when I fucking plug it in.'"

"Oh, right," he said. "That. You know, if I could go back and smack past me on the head with a brick—"

"Within current technological frameworks, I don't think you can." His partner swore under his breath and clicked frantically with his mouse. It was a moment before he resumed the conversation. "However, you do have the opportunity to make sure your future self doesn't have the same problems by being more responsible in the present."

"Hey, now." Jacob popped his head up over the edge of the desk and gave his friend a look. "Let's not take it too far, man."

"How did I know you'd say that?" Nick wore a pained expression.

"Because you've worked with him for years." Amber came to wrap her arms around Nick's shoulders and give him a sunny smile. "And we love him despite the fact that OSHA would shut this mess down in five seconds."

"That won't be a problem…" Jacob plugged a cord in and looked around to see the lights activate on another pod. "As long as no one snitches."

She mimed zipping her lips and throwing the key away. "Oh, but I should point out that even if no one snitches to OSHA, Justin's parents will soon be here."

"What was the point of zipping your lips if you weren't going to, you know…actually zip it?"

"Fine. Next time, I'll let you get caught with your pants down." She returned to her desk. "And in five minutes, when you've moved past your stubborn insistence on resolving it yourself, Nick and I will help."

"Speak for yourself." Nick launched into another flurry of clicks. "I have a fairy egg to rescue."

"You can pause the game," Jacob called from under the desk. "It's the space bar."

"First of all, I want to have something to show Mrs. Williams when she arrives. Second of all, the AI knows when I pause it and gets all snide when I come back." He hunkered in his chair. "And it's mean, you guys. Yesterday, it leveled up my Darwin Was Wrong skill to three and told me I was in the running to be the stupidest person on the server."

"Yeah…" Amber rolled back in her chair to look at the screen. "We're gonna want to fix that before Mrs. Williams logs in. Although, knowing her, she'll find how to make it be nice to her."

"My money's on that one," Jacob agreed. "Son of a bitch. I swear to God this cord has three ends."

She checked her watch and looked at Nick. "Three minutes and twenty seconds until he taps out. Be ready."

Nick snickered. His character, who currently ran through a tunnel made of glowing blue rock, tripped and sprawled heavily. **CLUMSY, LEVEL 8**, the screen told him, and he rolled his eyes.

"It's not my fault you keep falling," the AI said in his earpiece.

"You know what, I bet if I went back and looked, I'd find out you put some polygons in my way just then," Nick retorted.

"You are such a sore loser. In fact—"

The screen froze.

"Augh…" He groaned and lowered his face into his hands. "It's an instanced level! You're smart enough to get this. Only people in Justin's level need to be held to the same timeline."

The AI made no reply.

"Did it freeze again?" Jacob asked sympathetically.

"Yes." He came to sit next to him with a sigh. "I know we're still a minute and a half ahead of schedule but let me help you with this." He began to sort through the cords. "Okay…well, the reason you think your cord has three ends is that you have one of mine. Gimme. No, not that one, *that* one—yes." He tugged at it. "Feed it through."

"The senator's plane just landed," Amber called across the room.

"Fuck—feed it through quickly." Nick looked around the room a little desperately. "We don't have much time."

"By the way, Nick, the game restarted." She leaned back in her chair to look at the screen. "Aaaaaand you're dead by pixie."

"Son of a—" He sighed. "Okay, clean-up first, then I'll respawn and I'll find a way to punt that AI into next week."

The computer dinged and she looked at it again. "You have two new skills—Inadvisable Threats and Skynet Protocol, both level one."

By the time Tad and Mary walked into the lab, it barely resembled the same place. Nick and Jacob had been busy bundling cords, which now lay tied together neatly and adhered to the floor with clearly marked pathways between them.

Still, the new arrivals looked around with wide eyes and worried expressions.

"What is all this?" Mary asked. "Is there a…problem?"

"Oh." Amber scanned the room. It looked so much neater than it had twenty minutes before that it was difficult to see the problem, and she studied it carefully with fresh eyes. After a moment, she realized that however neat the arrangement of server blocks and cords might be, the area did look more like a server room than a medical facility. Even the lighting had been dimmed to keep the temperature in the room down and only the light directly above Justin's pod was on.

It looked like something out of a dystopian sci-fi film.

She bit her lip. "Oh, dear."

"I'm sure it's all fine," Tad said comfortingly. He squeezed his wife's arm. "I've seen many places in a panic, my dear, and this doesn't seem to be one. As long as they aren't panicked—"

The unmistakable sound of a zap and an exclamation cut him off in mid-assurance, and all the lights went out except the LEDs on Justin's pod. A large generator roared to life in the distance and the lights flickered on a moment later in time to reveal DuBois, who wandered from behind a stack of servers with his hair sticking up on end.

"Sorry about that," he said vaguely. "Wrong plug. I'll fix it."

"Wait, your hair *actually* stands up on end when you get shocked?" Nick looked at Amber in disbelief.

"I don't think that's the takeaway here." She pivoted to the Williams and plastered a smile on her face. "As DuBois demonstrated for us, we now have a chain of independent backup generators as well as a battery within Justin's pod. Any disruption to the main power grid will have no effect on its function, and if everything else is shut off, we have thirty-six hours of power to the pod if we need it."

Tad's mouth twitched and she thought he was enjoying this more than his wife. "I see."

"Now, Mrs. Williams." Amber guided the woman to the table where Nick had been playing the video game. "We've perfected the controls so that you can also play the video game. Because we know your primary purpose isn't to play, though, we're working to set a number of teleport points so you can move your character to wherever Justin is in order to speak to him. You also have an invulnerability buff—ah, like armor? Yes—and are universally coded as not being a threat. Nothing will attack you."

From the look on Mary's face, she hadn't considered the idea that she would need to play the game.

"One of the issues we can't control," the engineer continued, "is Justin's sleep and wake cycles, as well as the speed with which he processes information. To make a long story short, having what he perceives as a brief conversation could take hours or days. We're working on a couple of fixes for that, although it seems like his reaction times are improving."

"Ah," Mary said. She cleared her throat. "Well, thank you very much. It seems as though all of you have been busy."

"We have." Jacob gave her a tired smile. "Thankfully, one of the express provisions given by our mystery donor was that we could spend as much on coffee as we needed to."

"Do you have any idea yet who it is?" Tad asked. His voice was a touch too casual and Amber began to see the strain in him.

"Not yet," she told him. "I've managed to find a few of the hospital's major donors as well as the causes they support, but I haven't found anyone who seems like a match."

"Of course," the senator said. "I should have known that would all be published somewhere."

She cleared her throat and hoped her cheeks weren't red. The truth was that, although the donors did need to be named, no dollar amount was required to be published. That information had been obtained via slightly—or wildly—less than legal means.

Thankfully, her two partners both knew her well enough to know that she needed them to break into the conversation at this particular moment.

"Justin's progress seems stable," Jacob reported. "The leaps ahead we saw him make a week ago have held. It wasn't an anomaly and seems, instead, to be real improvement."

Thankfully, the couple was diverted.

"So he's getting better," Mary said. She looked relieved.

"There has been no forward progress since then," DuBois said and appeared at exactly the wrong time to offer the unvarnished truth. He studied his blackened fingers before he looked up to see everyone staring at him. "Jacob is quite right, the progress is indisputable and a holding pattern is good."

"It's…good?" The woman didn't seem to believe him.

"Asking for more right now would be like…" He raised his shoulders in a surprisingly artful shrug. "Asking someone with a new hip to walk a half-marathon. They could probably do it in extremis, but it would set their healing back. Slow and steady is what you want."

"Ah." Both of Justin's parents nodded.

"And how are matters on your end?" Nick asked them politely. "Senator, we caught a piece of your speech earlier. It was quite well-articulated."

"Thank you." But Tad's smile had disappeared entirely. "Unfortunately…it looks like we may have a complication soon. The media has caught wind of some part of this. I don't know how, exactly, although I have my suspicions, and I don't know how much they know. But I can tell you how they're spinning it. The insinuation is that this procedure hasn't received FDA approval because it is dangerous and that I know it's dangerous but decided to pull him out of the hospital and have you experiment on him."

Amber covered her face with her hands.

"Oh, no," Jacob managed to croak.

The only sound in the room was DuBois crunching popcorn. When everyone looked at him, he shrugged.

"Wasn't all of this already happening?" he asked. He shrugged. "They had the project blocked last time and they threatened to blackmail the senator. The difference is that now, we have funds to keep going."

Amber stared at him.

"He's right." Mary's voice was low and clear. "Thank you, Dr. DuBois. We all knew they would try to give us bad press, but we also know this is the best course for Justin and many other patients. We need to keep working—although I realize I shouldn't include myself in that. Nick, would you mind showing me some of the fundamentals of the game?"

Amber stood aside as the group swung into action once more. DuBois was right that this wasn't anything new.

On the other hand, it reminded her exactly how uncomfortable she was about the fact that their donor was still a mystery.

CHAPTER TWO

"Is everyone ready?" Lyle stroked his bushy beard and looked at Zaara and Justin.

"One moment." She rearranged her cards.

"Come on, human. How long can it take you to read those? You've had 'em all in your hand." Lyle shook his head at Justin. He added in a stage whisper, "I'm starting to think she's not too bright."

"There's no need to be rude," Zaara said mildly and for a moment, Justin thought he could see the young gold digger her father had tried to raise with perfect manners and an artful tilt to her head. "After all, this is a new game for me. Oh! What's that?" She pointed across the tavern.

"What?" Lyle turned to look, and the young man watched with weary amusement as she switched several cards between her hand and the dwarf's. A ball of multicolored light danced in the corner of the tavern to which she'd pointed.

Lyle drank his beer while he watched with a slight frown and when the bright globe faded, he looked at the table. "I dunno why that keeps happening, but it sure is pretty. Wait...hic...you can see it, too, right?"

"Yes." Zaara did not mention that she had pointed it out in the first place.

Or, as Justin could plainly see, that she had been the one who created it. She was smiling, all innocence, as she laid her cards out on the table. "Is this a good hand? I wasn't sure so I bet low."

"Never tell people why ye bet the way ye do," the dwarf said. He looked at her hand, narrowed his eyes, and looked at his. "Wait. I had that card."

"Are there two of them in the deck?" she asked and laid the innocence on with a spatula.

"No, I had it in my hand." He gave her a hard look.

"You had it in your hand in the *last* round," Zaara told him. "Remember?"

Lyle swayed in his seat and hiccupped. "Yeah. Yeah, I guess you're right."

"Unbelievable," Justin muttered. A moment later, her boot connected with his shin and he winced. "Ow!"

"Eh?" The dwarf gave him a look. "Did you get hurt killing that wizard, Justin me boy?"

"No," he said. "I'm merely marveling at Zaara's luck this evening. *Ow!*" He rubbed his shin and glared at her. "Also, I seem to keep hitting my shin on this table."

"How sad," she said sweetly. "You haven't shown your hand, by the way. Maybe you won."

"Yes." Justin took a sip of his beer. He had almost adjusted to the fact that the game's graphics didn't show the beer moving when he moved the mug—and the fact that he could only half-taste the beer. It was only a memory of what it tasted like, after all. He laid his cards down. "Ah, no. Lost again. How sad. You know, it doesn't seem to be my night. I think I'll bow out and watch you two play."

SORE LOSER, LEVEL 2 popped up on the screen and he rolled his eyes. It might be his imagination, but it seemed like the AI had been snarkier than usual.

"Eh," Lyle said. He slid a small pile of coins to Zaara. "That's the last turn for me or I won't have any for my next pint. This one's having all the beginner's luck."

"Yeah, that's what it is," he responded blandly. This time, however, he lifted his legs out of the way as she kicked and was rewarded by the sound of a boot hitting the chair leg and her muttered oath of pain. "Is there a problem, Zaara?"

"No," she said, with dignity. "I'm fine. Thank you."

"You're welcome." He grinned and put his feet down.

POKER FACE, LEVEL 1 the game announced. **REALLY BAD FLIRTING, LEVEL 1.**

"I am not flirting," he whispered under his breath. His cheeks flamed suddenly.

"What?" Zaara looked at him. From her expression, it seemed as if she genuinely hadn't heard him.

"Uh…I said… That's not…Murting."

"Who's Murting?"

"Someone I know." Justin hastened to extricate himself from the conversation. "Hey, look over there—oh. Hey. Look over there." To his utter surprise—and relief—something *was* going on. The town crier had come in with the week's new bounties, each stamped with a seal of approval from the mayor's office.

A few chairs scraped, and assorted people stood to peer at the new posters. Sephith, the wizard who once ruled this valley, had attracted a steady stream of adventurers, and over the past week, several had arrived in East Newbrook. With him now defeated, they were all looking for alternate employment.

Justin hadn't seen Zaara leave the table but a moment later, she sat and slid a piece of paper across the table. "I took the best one," she said with a wink.

Had that wink always made his stomach flip? He shook his head to clear it. She wasn't real and was merely a collection of pixels run by an AI who hated him. With his luck, she would ask him out as a joke and he'd be laughed at by an entire pixelated village.

He took a moody sip of his beer and wished it were real before he took the piece of paper to read.

"Ruins. That could be good."

"*Could* be good?" Zaara flipped her hand and uncurled her fingers to show the key they had salvaged from Sephith's castle. "There are three keys. We have one and no one's even heard tell of the other two for years. Ruins might be the only place to start tracking things like that."

"As long as there's loot, I'm in," Lyle interjected. He hiccupped. "I'll go get more beer."

"He's right. You're right." Justin blew a breath out. The group had scrounged a few minor missions but nothing that paid well, and at this point, they barely covered their stay at the inn. "We should go to the ruins. But…" He held a finger up. "We should also get a few smaller jobs with easy payouts—something to fall back on."

"Those are so boring." She tossed a piece of bread in the air and caught it in her mouth.

"Your first mission was defeating a necromancer wizard, but they won't all be like that, you know." He raised his eyebrows at her. "Mark my words, you'll find out that adventuring is equally as boring as the life you ran away from."

"Really?" She leaned forward on her crossed arms. "You think adventuring will become as boring as sitting in a backwater nowhere village, doing needlework and practicing my giggle to impress a nobleman."

"Um…" He had to admit she had a point.

With a grin, Zaara hurried to the board and pulled down another few jobs. She returned and waved them under his nose. "A missing wedding ring and a wolf going after sheep. I hope that's boring enough for you, Sir…"

"Sir…" Justin prompted.

"I can't think of anything." She sounded annoyed. "Dammit, and I wanted it to be such a good insult." She looked up as Lyle joined them. "Lyle, we're going to do tiny adventures."

The dwarf gave her a dubious look and hiccupped, but he shrugged. He was not, the young man noticed, carrying another mug of beer. The bartender must have guessed that he wouldn't see any coin for it.

"I'll go," Lyle said. "And by the way, when will we go back to Riverbend for that ten gold? I've told people about the money I'll have coming in, and it'll be good if, you know…I can pay them for things. We defeated the wizard."

Justin rolled his eyes. "Yes, but the Mayor won't pay us."

"He won't?" The dwarf looked outraged.

"The reward," he said patiently, "was for rescuing Zaara and she doesn't want to go back."

"Trust me," she said, "he wouldn't pay you anyway. He only put up the sign so someone would come to East Newbrook, find me, and drag me back. Then he'd string you along and smooth-talk you. Believe me when I say you two aren't missing out on anything."

"I still think he should pay us," Lyle grumbled.

"You haven't been in this business long, have you?" Justin asked him. He stood. "Either way, we won't get that money tonight and we need to pay for our stay at the inn. How about we go see the farmer and kill that wolf?"

The dwarf followed them as they headed out into the night. He muttered quietly, as much to himself and an imaginary audience of other dwarves as to his companions, so the other two ignored him.

"I'm sorry my father's a jerk," Zaara said after a while. "I know ten gold would help you."

"Yeah," Justin said absently. "I don't know. I guess I don't understand why you're still here, though."

"What do you mean?" She walked with her hands resting on the hilts of her daggers.

What do I mean? He had no idea, and as he tried to find the answer, he made the mistake of starting to talk. Some people could come up with a nice speech on the fly, but he was not one of them.

"It's dangerous out here, that's all."

"You don't mind," she pointed out.

"I'm stuck here, remember?"

"Oh, right." Zaara shook her head. "I keep thinking that one of these days, we'll see a poster with your picture on it and it'll say some madman escaped."

The AI snickered.

"Are you laughing at your own joke?" Justin asked under his breath. "Seriously? Come on." To her, he added, "Very funny. First of all, that's clearly Lyle."

She snorted with laughter.

"Second of all," he continued, "you don't have to believe me. I don't expect you to. It's merely…true."

"If it were true, wouldn't you sit around, drink beer, and wait to wake up?" she asked practically.

"I don't know. It seems not." He rolled his eyes. "Why don't you?"

"Oh, you are insufferable." Zaara drew her knives.

"Whoa! Hey!"

"Justin." She waved the knives at him. "Look over there."

Justin turned to look and stopped in his tracks. A massive shadow slunk around the tree line nearby and toward a pasture where he could see sheep grazing. As it moved into a gap in the shadows, the moonlight glinted off brindled fur.

"Oh, shit," he said. "Are we sure that's not a…you know…bear?"

"Wolves are big. I thought you knew that." Zaara set off briskly. "Come on, Lyle, we have a rabid wolf to kill."

"It's rabid?" He followed her and unsheathed his sword. The animal moved more quickly now and they increased their pace slightly.

"We haven't exactly been quiet," she called over her shoulder. "And it's still there, so either it's starving—which is not the case—or it's rabid."

"The lady has a point." Lyle brushed past him, his fists readied.

"I'm not a lady," she told him crossly.

"She has a point about that, too," the dwarf agreed.

"Are you going to punch a wolf?" he asked as he hurried behind them. He had a bad feeling about this wolf. Zaara was right. It should be able to hear them and it didn't seem to care at all that they were there.

The bleating of the lambs made his mind up for him. One of them trotted to its mother in the moonlight and he immediately broke into a run. There were lambs in this field and sheep that did not have a chance in hell against this monster wolf from hell. He did not intend to sit around and watch pixelated sheep die. His unease pushed aside, he held one hand out and prepared to throw a fireball—

"Are you crazy?" Zaara caught him as he moved past, held his sword arm out the way, and tripped him. "Fireballs in a pasture?"

"Ow," Justin said. "Listen, I—"

"Stooooooooooooout!"

Justin and Zaara exchanged a glance before she yanked him to his feet and they sprinted after Lyle. They hurdled the fence and pushed through the herd of sheep, all of whom seemed determined to put themselves firmly in the way.

To their teammate's credit, the wolf seemed as surprised as they were. The beast had stopped at the edge of the meadow in a larger patch of shadow than those around it, and seemed to be under the impression that no one would be stupid enough to run directly up to it and punch it in the nose.

It had not bargained on Lyle Stout, who did exactly that. After a surprised yelp, the wolf backed away and snarled suddenly. It snapped its teeth and padded forward.

With a low growl, it slunk away again as Justin tumbled over the second fence and narrowly missed impaling himself on his sword. He rolled, ended on his feet, and swiped his hand to clear the **CLUMSY, LEVEL 8** that flashed up on the screen.

The wolf now stared dubiously at him, and he didn't wait for it to recover. He went on the offensive at once with a battle cry. Over and over, he brought the sword down to slash, and thrust, and wave it like a battle-ax.

It wasn't a winning strategy, but it didn't have to be. The wolf continued its retreat and backed away step by step, so it seemed to be working.

In the next moment, Zaara barreled into it from the side. She tumbled over it and one of her knives found flesh. The animal opened its mouth in a snarl of pain, but the light was already fading from its eyes. It slumped heavily and she heaved herself free.

"Good job," she said, panting. "See? One wolf, no big deal."

"Hey!" The call came from across the field. A man hurried toward them dressed in the baggy, patched clothes of a villager. "Are you from East Newbrook? Did you kill the wolf?"

"We did," Justin said. He panted as he sheathed his sword.

"My thanks, my thanks." The farmer reached them and looked at each of the adventurers in turn. "There's a purse for you to split and another half to be given by the mayor. He knew once the wolf had finished with my flocks, he'd look for others." He held the purse out to Justin. "And there's something else for the lady."

"I'm not a lady," Zaara muttered.

The farmer smiled and withdrew something from under his shirt. It was wrapped in heavy fabric and he opened it as gently as if it were a baby. Nestled in the black cloth was a well-worn sheath and one of the most beautiful daggers Justin had ever seen.

She drew her breath sharply.

"It was my grandfather's," the farmer said. "I never had the training for it, and he was a wild soul—wouldn't like it being used for sheep shearing or a kitchen knife or naught like that. When I heard an adventurer was in town with daggers, I thought maybe I'd sell it. But you saved my flocks and because of you, my children will eat this winter. Have this knife. My grandfather would want that."

"Thank you," she whispered as she picked it up. "Oh, thank you. It's beautiful."

"If he were still alive," the man said, "he'd have gone after Sephith, himself, no matter that he was ninety and blind. Go. Free other towns."

"I will be honored to use this," Zaara told him, and for the first time, Justin saw something in her face and thought he understood why she didn't want to go home. This was the kind of story she would never hear if she were a nobleman's wife.

He was silent as they walked to town, sad without knowing why.

CHAPTER THREE

Birds chirped merrily the next morning when Justin awoke. He took a moment to stretch before he remembered that he wasn't stretching for any reason. This game could mimic many things, but one it didn't—hopefully by design—was the way you could toss and turn in your sleep or wake up with a crick in your neck.

"You awaken feeling well-rested," he murmured as he sat. He pushed the shutters open to see the bird that trilled so happily. It turned to look at him, chirped, and failed to notice the drifting, magical ember on the wind.

The change was rapid—the bird ignited and the flames swelled and twisted with darkness. It uttered a low cry that pierced him to the bone and collapsed into a puddle of greenish goo below the window with a muted plop.

He sat with his hand over his mouth.

"I gotta do something about that," he muttered hoarsely when he had recovered enough to talk. Although Sephith had been defeated, he had ruled the valley for years and the residue of his battle to take the tower remained—a kind of magical fallout that could sicken people, crops, and livestock. He had seen more than a few villagers with withered limbs or burns on their faces and shoulders. This was the only place where people wore their hoods down in the rain and up in the sunshine.

Downstairs, the innkeeper was serving beans, cheese, and bread to Zaara and Lyle. Justin narrowed his eyes and looked more closely. The innkeeper was serving her only, and she had decided to sit at the same table where Lyle had passed out the night before.

Justin smiled as he joined her. "How are we saving the world today?"

"First, we're eating breakfast. Do you want some?" She tipped her plate of beans at him.

They looked way too similar to the bird-goo and his stomach heaved.

Zaara raised her eyebrows. "I've never seen that look on a man before. You're not a woman, are you? Secretly with child?" She ducked under the table to peer at his stomach.

"I'm not a woman," he said in annoyance. "But…no beans. Bread."

"Right." She scooped a spoonful into her mouth and laughed at the look on his face. "Well, don't look. But do eat. We'll need our strength."

"I thought—thank you—" Justin accepted a hunk of bread from the innkeeper, along with a mug of something that was vaguely tea-like if tea were made with pond scum. "Ew. I thought we were retrieving a wedding ring?"

"Sure, but first we have to drag Lyle out to the fountain and dunk his head in until he wakes up." Zaara took a sip of her tea. "Try it. Despite appearances, it's good."

He sipped it, winced, and was surprised to find that it tasted a little like a smoothie—fruity and chalky at the same time, but warm. He could work with that, he decided.

Once they had finished, he took a piece of bread to go on Lyle's account, and he and Zaara dunked the dwarf successfully under the water a few times before the three of them set off toward the edge of town. Justin waited for Zaara to ask how he always knew where to go, but she never did. It was a shame, he thought. He'd looked forward to explaining the concept of a mini-map.

The widow lived in a surprisingly picturesque little cottage. He was sure that if he stood close enough, he'd be able to identify the pixels, but he'd taken considerable flak from his teammates about that before.

Justin knocked on the door, and it wasn't long before the widow opened it. She was bright-eyed and vibrant but frail.

"Adventurers," she said with a smile. "Are you here for potions? Could I interest you in a quest?"

"To find your wedding ring?" Zaara asked. "If so, that is why we came. We wanted to find it for you."

"Oh, bless you, children." The woman smiled and waved them to a table.

The interior of the cottage was spotless, with copper pans and ladles on the walls, a small bed with a quilted bedspread, and a merry fire in the grate. A thin workbench on the other wall was packed with bottles and herbs, a scale, and a mortar and pestle. Onions hung from the rafters in bunches and braided rag rugs covered the floor.

"I was near the sewer grates," the widow explained. "Up on the king's highway, you know. We have nothing so fine here in East Newbrook, of course." She laughed.

Justin, who had never considered a sewer to be a cause for celebration, forced a smile.

"Well, Sweetgrass grows out of the sewer grates, and as I stretched in to harvest a clump, my wedding ring fell off." She turned over a piece of paper that had lain on the table. "I marked the location very carefully. It's the grate fourteen paces west of the 485th league marker."

"Okay." He looked at his two companions and was pleased to

see them both nodding. Someone, at least, seemed to know where they were going.

"I'd go find it myself, you see, except these old bones wouldn't take that very well."

She shook her head with a laugh. "And I'd wait, but the same old bones tell me there's a storm coming. Where there's a storm, there's water, and any chance of finding my ring will be gone."

"Of course." Zaara picked the piece of paper up and smiled. "We'll be back with your ring, ma'am."

"He seems to be making friendships," DuBois remarked.

"Hmm?" Amber looked up from her ledgers.

"Justin." The doctor gestured at the screens. "He's bonding with the characters in the game. He wants to keep them from getting hurt."

"It isn't surprising. Did you know a study was done with robots that looked nothing close to human, and the human test subjects still refused to destroy them? They didn't want to 'hurt' them." She smiled. "Humans will pack-bond with anything."

"Maybe." He didn't seem convinced. "Sure, he could have simply wandered around, pushed people into lakes, or swung his sword every which way, and I tend to think many people might do that—sudden freedom from social judgment, after all, and no consequences. But Zaara was right—he could also have holed up in a tavern and refused to interact."

"I was worried he would when we sent his parents' message through," she admitted, looked at her research, and sighed. She was getting nowhere fast so might as well take a proper break. "I thought if he knew there was a real chance of dying, he might simply stop trying and we'd have to back him into a corner."

"That wouldn't have been pleasant for anyone," DuBois said. He nodded at her work. "I'm sorry to have taken you from that.

You did sigh almost continuously, though. I thought perhaps you could use a distraction."

"Thank you." She was always surprised when he did something human, although she had begun to think he was the type to observe carefully and interact more fully once he knew people. He now picked up everyone else's favorite snacks at the grocery store too, and if he was listening to jazz—which Nick couldn't stand—he always turned it off before the man was due to arrive for the day.

"Is there a problem?" the doctor asked.

"Well…" Amber gestured for him to approach her desk. With all the new equipment, she had moved from the center of the big room to one of the corners. She pointed at the screen. "I can find nothing that tells me who this benefactor is, and the timing is—"

"What timing?"

"When this all leaked to the press?" She raised her eyebrows and pulled her phone out of her pocket to show him. "Look— forty-eight missed calls. My old roommate's getting calls and my classmates are getting calls. I emailed the people at your lab and they told me they've had to unplug their phones."

"Ah, yes." He nodded his head seriously. "This is why I don't have a phone."

"What if someone needs to reach you?"

He shrugged. "My lab knows where I am. And the truth would come out sometime, wouldn't it? The press is always looking for something. The only thing that surprises me is that more details haven't emerged yet. They aren't very good at looking, are they?"

Amber could only laugh at that. DuBois was a man whose career had almost been ended by these same forces, and he was offended on a personal level that the people who tried to destroy them weren't better at their jobs.

"Well, why don't you see if you can resolve this puzzle." She pulled the chair out for him. "Justin's sleeping, after all, and—"

"And?" DuBois looked at her with a small frown. "What's—"

"Here's all the info." She tapped the screen. "Read it and let it sink in."

She took a careful step and sank to the floor before she slunk around the maze of desks and cords. While not exactly a ninja, she could move quietly when she needed to and the hums and beeps of the machinery covered her movement.

DuBois muttered to himself as she eased out from behind a desk, took a look at the server wall, and shook her head.

Stealth.

And speed.

And don't destroy the servers. She stood as quietly as she could, took two long, quiet steps, and put the intruder she'd seen in a headlock. The camera tumbled free and she kicked it with every ounce of strength she possessed so it skidded into the darkened interior of the room. The intruder, meanwhile, screamed.

"What's going on?" Across the room, DuBois stood with a horrified look. "Who is that?"

"A reporter, I think." Amber flipped the woman over her shoulder and onto the floor, where she yanked her hands up behind her and knelt on her back. "I'm right, aren't I? You're a reporter?"

"This is assault," the woman said shrilly.

"Oh, no." She hauled her up. "How terrible for you. You snuck into private property to try to take pictures of trade secrets, potentially disrupting experiments in progress, and with what goal, exactly?"

"The world deserves to know the truth about Justin Williams," her captive said as Amber began to force her down the hallway.

"Who?"

"You know exactly who I mean. He's in that…that pod thing, isn't he?"

"To be clear, you think there's a missing person in our lab and you've decided the best way to save him is to come in and look at our server blocks?" She shook her head, kicked the outside door open, and ushered the woman firmly into the sunlight. "Here's a fun suggestion. Why don't you...I don't know, do your research and find out who we are before you sneak onto our property. There's also a doorbell." She slammed the door, locked it from the inside, and walked away, ignoring the woman's shouts about her camera.

In the lab, DuBois stood and stared worriedly at the door. "Are you sure you should have done that?" he asked.

"Yes," she said. "Did you make any progress with the information?"

"There's hardly enough to make sense of," he said with a shrug. "We'll have to wait until—oh, look, he's waking up." He snatched a bag of popcorn and headed to the monitors, and Amber laughed ruefully before she returned to her computer.

Whether this was enough information or not, the reporter's visit had shown her one thing. They needed to identify the players in this game and they needed to do it fast. Not for the first time, she wished she could swap places with Justin.

If she had to fight mysterious strangers, she'd rather have a sword and some fireballs.

The King's Road was like an entirely different world. Justin had become familiar with the villages and dirt paths, but the big road half a league away was made of shining white stone. Weeds grew here and there, of course, but in general, it was in remarkably good repair.

"People come every year to clean it," Zaara explained. "And reset the cobbles and all that. You can see who did which parts— the stones are all engraved with who was ruling when the stone was laid. So...look, most of these are from Hieronymous, who was the first one to extend the King's Road out this way, but this stone is more recent."

"Huh." Justin shrugged. "Chipping the King's name into thousands of cobblestones seems like…maybe a waste of time?"

"The kings don't think so," she said and mirrored his shrug.

"The kings don't have to do it, I assume. Okay, there's the bridge and the mile marker, so we have to go west of that—or east?"

"West." Zaara picked out the small grey stone at the edge of the road. "I'll go count the steps." Lyle and Justin waited as she approached the marker and counted the required number of steps before she laughed in triumph. "Ha! Right where she said it would be. Now, I guess we need to find a way to get this grate up."

"Let me." Lyle marched to her, felt under the stone, and gave a satisfied grunt. He pulled his knife out and stuck it under the grate. Stone and steel scraped together jarringly before he hauled the cover up and threw it into the grass. "There it goes. It's a dwarven make and locked in so someone can't simply take a nice hunk of iron, eh? Anyhow, in we gooooo!" He sat on the edge of the opening, pushed off, and disappeared. The sound of boots hitting wet stone followed moments later.

"Did we even check to see if the ring was simply there?" Justin asked.

"Nope," Zaara said. She sighed as she leaned over. "I don't see it, though. You know, I'm not looking forward to this." She levered herself down more carefully, then called, "It's barely a drop for a human, don't worry!"

He was surprised to feel a few stabs of pain in his arms as he swung down. That had happened sometimes lately, and he wondered if it was actual pain in broken limbs—the thought made him shudder—or merely biofeedback that had been fouled up in the system.

As always, the thought of his own sleeping body made him nervous. and he decided to think about something else. The truly terrible smell in the sewer was first on the list.

"Lyle?"

"Over this way."

"How do you know you're going the right direction?"

"Put a dwarf underground and ask 'im to find gold, and he won't fail ye."

The two humans looked at one another, shrugged, and headed off, following the sound of his voice. He did, in fact, seem remarkably good at leading them through the passages of the sewer, most of which were blessedly dry.

"Lyle," he said.

"Eh?"

"You can…get us out again, right?"

The dwarf scratched his ear. "Uh…yeah. Yeah, sure."

"We'll die down here," Justin told Zaara. "Either that or we'll turn into Morlocks."

"Into what?"

"Nothing. I—oh, hey, is that—oh, no." He raced forward to yank on the back of Lyle's shirt. At the end of the tunnel, a shaft of light from another sewer grate illuminated the edge of a glittering pile. It wasn't all treasure, but there were coins mixed in with the battered knives and slivers of glass.

A scrabbling sound came from somewhere nearby, followed by sniffing.

He drew his sword, Zaara drew her knives, and Lyle edged forward with his fists ready.

"One…" he whispered.

"Two…" Zaara continued."

"Stoooooooout!" Lyle yelled as he attacked.

"Oh, for—" Justin surged into a sprint. "Leeroooooooy!" He came around the corner and slashed at the first thing he saw that wasn't Lyle.

Between the squealing, dodging dwarf and making sure he didn't trip on the metal, it took him a while to identify what he was fighting—a truly giant rat. He had never seen anything like it if the truth be told. Its eyes glinted red, its fur was thick and mangy, and its teeth looked longer than any animal's had a right to be.

"This rodent," Justin yelled as he backed out of the way of the snapping teeth, "is a truly unusual size."

"Oh, you noticed, did you?" Zaara shouted in response.

"R!" he called as he slashed. "O! U!" He stepped forward and thrust the blade into the animal's eye. "S!"

It screamed and fell to the ground, where it twitched horribly.

"ROUS?" Zaara asked blankly.

"So, it's not a human thing?" Lyle asked her.

"No. No, it's not."

"It's a long story." Justin shrugged. "Oh, hey, look." He stooped to take a gold ring off the ground. "It was hoarding things like a dragon. Off we go, I guess."

"Will you tell us about the ROUS?" Zaara asked. "We do have quite a walk ahead of us, after all."

"Fine, fine… Okay, so where do I begin? Once, there was a princess named Buttercup…"

<hr>

It had begun to get dark by the time they reached the widow's hut again, and when she hobbled to the door, it was with a radiant smile.

"So you found my ring! Oh, children, let me get your reward." She hobbled away but returned quickly with a coin purse and a bag that clinked like glass. "I made you all some salves and potions."

"Thank you," Zaara said humbly. "Would you look at Justin's arm? He's tried not to let us see but it had a nasty bite."

"Of course, of course." The woman beckoned them to the table and fixed Justin with a look. "Now, let me see. Ah, good God. Child, this wound is poisoning you."

"Er…" He had seen the bleed debuff as it chipped away at his health and expected it to go away. So far, though, it hadn't. "Yes."

"And did it not occur to you to ask for help?" She clicked her teeth, hobbled to the table in the corner, and began mixing. "One of these days, that'll kill you."

"I'd say it's more important that he learn how to dodge," Zaara suggested.

"You're too clumsy," the AI told Justin. *"I keep waiting for you to figure out your role but you don't. This is excruciating."*

"Excruciating for you?" he muttered under his breath. "I'm the one with the bite on my arm."

"Look, you don't have what it takes to do all the fancy footwork. Try something else."

Justin didn't have a chance to ask what it meant as the healer had returned with a set of salves and bandages. Zaara carried a steaming bowl of water.

"Hold him," the older woman told the other two.

"What? Hold me? Why—ow, fuck!" He did his very best to levitate through the roof of the thatched-roof cottage, an effort that was thwarted by his teammates. They hung onto him as the woman cleaned the wound with brisk, efficient strokes of a brush and rubbed the whole area with salve. "God in heaven, woman, what are you doing?"

She didn't bother to answer. "Keep holding him," she told his companions. She bound the wound tightly with strips of linen and stooped to glare at him. "If I have them release you, will you leave the bandage on?"

"My arm," he said through gritted teeth, "is on fire."

"Good gracious, boy, you can see that's not true." She looked at his companions. "Give it a few more seconds."

"I'll give you all my loot," Justin said wildly to Lyle. To Zaara, he suggested, "And a new set of daggers. Maybe? An old map? Uh…a magic textbook?"

"I'd like that." She gave him that smile that made his stomach flip. "But I won't let go of you. Sit still and stop being such a baby."

Hearing her call him a baby wasn't good for his wounded pride. Justin sank into the chair and muttered under his breath, but he noticed that the wound had begun to feel better. He watched the widow darkly as she went to the corner and pulled something out from under the bed. When she turned holding a sword, he almost shoved the chair over backward as visions of demonic sacrifice ran rampant in his head. Even Lyle and Zaara surged to their feet.

Their hostess gave them a disbelieving look. "Good heavens. I'm not planning to kill you. I want to give you this sword. It's a good sight better than the one you have, and gods know, I've no use for it. Now, run along, all of you. It's getting late and you need your rest if you plan to go off adventuring. Remember to come back for potions."

It was surprisingly pleasant to have an annoying parent in the game too. Justin smiled at her and bowed awkwardly. When she handed him the sword, it felt heavy in his hands but also right. This was the kind he'd wanted when he started the game, and no amount of polishing would make his old, rusted blade into a proper weapon like this one.

"Thank you," he told the woman. "We'll be back, I promise."

CHAPTER FOUR

The villagers of East Newbrook had heard of the good deeds the three adventurers had done. Justin almost thought they cared more about the lost wedding ring and the flocks of sheep than they did about Sephith's defeat.

"Of course they do," Zaara said over a lavish breakfast. The innkeeper had only reluctantly taken coin for their rooms the night before and now went out of his way to offer every amenity he could.

"I don't get it." Justin took a big bite of bread. If he didn't concentrate too hard, he really could imagine he was eating.

"Look." She considered what to say for a moment. "There are always tyrants, right? There's always some fuckhead wanting to rule the world who turns villagers into slaves. If it hadn't been Sephith, it'd probably have been the king, drafting them to fight in his wars. Sure, they hated that dude, but as far as they're concerned, another one will simply come along soon."

He put his mug of ale down and stared at her. "Are you telling me we went through all of that for nothing, in their opinion?"

"Not nothing." She shrugged. "They're always happy to see someone like that defeated. But they know that soon, there'll be another one. When it comes to things like lost wedding rings or wolf packs…well, you can deal with those. Once you fix those problems, everyone's better off for a while."

"Huh." He ate a few berries off his plate while he it though. "I never thought of it like that."

"That's plain." Zaara gave him a curious look. "Where do you come from that you don't know anyone who thinks like that?"

Justin decided against even trying to explain Silicon Valley. "It's a long story and not as cool as the one about Princess Buttercup. Let's go find Lyle and dunk him in the fountain."

"Your dwarf friend is already up," the innkeeper informed them. "He got up with the sun and he's at the blacksmith. He said he was looking for something for you."

"For me?" He exchanged a confused glance with his teammate. "I guess we'd better go see, then. We're heading to the ruins today, so we won't be back for a while."

"I'll have my boy run some provisions to the blacksmith," the landlord told them. "And your rooms will be kept ready, don't you fear."

He would have protested but Zaara shook her head. As they walked out into the sunlight, she told him, "Tyrants are common, but heroes are rare. East Newbrook saw many adventurers come through looking for glory and almost none of them cared to help with the little things." She elbowed him. "Besides, weren't you excited to have tavern wenches falling all over you?"

"Uh…" He colored and cleared his throat awkwardly. That fantasy now seemed embarrassingly juvenile. His dreams lately had been filled not so much with curvy tavern wenches as a figure in black armor, light on her feet and with a ready smile. "Someone pointed out that was stupid."

"Eh." She shrugged. "Well, I'll be damned, the innkeeper was right." She pointed to where Lyle lounged outside the blacksmith's shop. "Lyle!"

"So ye finally decided to show up." The dwarf shook his head at them. "Lazy buggers."

"This coming from the dwarf who wakes up at noon most days," Justin said. "The innkeeper said you were here getting something for...me?"

"That's right." He slung his arm around the young man's shoulders. Given the difference in their heights, it didn't work very well and he settled for shoving him in the back to push him into the blacksmith's shop. "My thought was what do ye do with someone who doesn't know how to avoid his enemies?"

"Footwork lessons?" he suggested.

"Oh, should I add tap dancing to this game?" the AI asked him.

"Nah, you're too hopeless for that." Lyle delivered the insult distractedly. He looked at the blacksmith, who hammered a large sheet of metal. "Armor!"

"Oh, wow." Justin dropped his pack on the floor and hurried to look. The armor was a little rough but it was miles better than anything he'd had yet. Between this and the new sword, it would be like playing an entirely different game.

The blacksmith, a young man with his hair held back in a braid, ducked his head apologetically. "It's not as good as it should be, sir. Our master blacksmith was taken by Sephith a year past, and no one worth their salt would come to replace him. I've made it so another should be able to add to it, though."

"Don't apologize." He looked at his leather armor. "This is what it's replacing, after all. And I like it. Did you teach yourself to do this?"

"I was still learning when Geoffrey was taken." The young man flushed. "And most of what these people need is nails and plows and so on. Horseshoes too, not armor or swords."

"I'm glad to have this." He began to strip his leather armor off. "Do you want any of this for scraps? And how much do I owe you?"

"Aye, the leather would be useful. It'll be…" The blacksmith swallowed. "Fifteen copper, sir."

It was a pitifully low price for his work and barely enough to cover the cost of the metal, and after a few days of adventures, Justin had enough in his purse to spend more. He handed him two silver as well as his leather armor and his old sword. With the blacksmith's thanks ringing in their ears, the adventurers clanked away to find an alchemist.

The new armor was difficult to walk in. He noticed fatigue taking his energy every few steps and could only hope that he grew stronger as time went on. Lyle took practice swipes with his new weapons—sets of long, curved claws that he wore over his knuckles. It would turn any normal boxing match into a bloodbath—and make the dwarf's punches less ridiculous and more deadly.

Although Justin had to admit, his teammate did have a very good track record due to sheer chutzpah. Few wolves, orcs, or wizards could believe that an unarmed dwarf would run in, headlong and with no apparent concern, to punch them.

The alchemist, a man with a long beard and overly dramatic phrasing, had several things in stock. He sold "a vial of the sea's fury" to Lyle—a basic potion Justin suspected was nothing more than caffeine—and "the purest, distilled essence of the stars" to Zaara.

"What exactly is that?" he asked her once they were out of the shop.

"I'll show you." She led him to a bench, where she wet a rag with the potion and rubbed it carefully over both her daggers. When she had finished, she put the bottle away with great care and placed the rag on the cobblestones before she stated, "Ignis!" The two blades and the rag both burst into flames and she smiled, satisfied. "See?"

"So, here's how it'll work," Lyle said, as they made their way out of town, their packs heavier now with the provisions from the innkeeper. "I'll run out and surprise 'em and Justin can follow and draw their attention with that sword. Once they're all focused on him, Zaara and I will do the real damage."

"Excuse me," Justin said, with dignity. "I can be useful, you know."

"Of course you can," she said soothingly. "And this is how. You take all the hits."

"Oh." He realized now what the AI had tried to push him toward. "I'll be the tank."

"Finally." He chose to ignore the comment and the snark in it.

"What's a tank?" Lyle asked.

"Uh…nothing. It's not important. Let's head to those ruins, shall we?"

Mary took the last sip of her coffee and looked around. Normally, Tad would be whistling while he read through his briefings for the day. He probably was, she reminded herself, but he was in DC right now and she was there to be close to Justin— which meant the house was unnaturally quiet.

She cleaned her breakfast dishes with a sigh and got ready to leave. DuBois and the others were sure that, any day now, she would be able to try to go into the game world with him, and she was equal parts impatient and terrified. She had only ever seen the pods used for comatose patients and even the thought of being put under was enough to worry her.

Her desire to see her son, however, was stronger than her fear. At the insistence of the doctor, she and Tad had not sent any further messages. They weren't supposed to distract him, the man explained. He needed to focus on strengthening himself and his survival instincts and forging relationships.

Those relationships were what worried her. She had seen him form very few close friendships in his life, and she had never seen him take to someone as quickly as he had bonded with Zaara. The woman might be a figment of his imagination, but Mary was quite sure no mother would be happy with her son bringing home a black-leather-clad, dagger-wielding runaway.

Not only that, a part of her had worried since she gave Justin the dragon that he would never want to return to the real world. Why would he, after all, when he had everything he'd ever wanted? Now, he could throw fireballs, run his life without any restrictions, and ride dragons. If he fell in love too, that could be too much to come back from.

She realized she simply stood and stared into nothing with the water pouring over her hands. With a little shake of her head, she put the mug and plate into the dishwasher and was about to pick her purse up when the computer dinged.

It was probably her sister, she thought. Ever since Justin's accident, the family had tried to rally around the two of them and even offered to fly out. When he was moved to the PIVOT labs, however, Mary had tried to keep them all at arm's length—an attempt that had fallen apart spectacularly when the press broke the story of the "experiments" being done on him.

While Tad dodged reporters in DC, she had dodged them at home as well as fielded increasingly worried questions from her family. She didn't like lying but she also knew that her family wouldn't understand the range of pressures that were being brought to bear on the Williamses.

If she didn't answer this email, though, her sister might well go a little insane and fly out from Nebraska, and she shuddered to think of that. She went to the computer, brought up her email, and her face immediately snapped into a glare.

It wasn't Annette who had emailed her. It was the girl who'd almost killed Justin and who was the reason they were in this mess to start with.

Mary had refused to see Tina in the hospital. She'd ignored the calls, the texts, and the handwritten letters. She had deleted the voicemails and text messages without reading them before she blocked the girl's number and shredded the letters. When Tad's aides called her to pass messages on, she told them not to speak to the woman.

How she had gotten her email, she didn't know. On the advice of other senate spouses, she had set up a new one when Tad was elected and it wasn't linked to anything—not any of her favorite shops, not the utilities, and not even her friends.

She was about to delete the message, but the title caught her eye. *Please*, it read simply.

Only one word and nothing more.

Something about that word caught at her heart and she swallowed. *Please.* She could sense Tina's desperation, and almost of its own volition, her hand scrolled slowly. She hesitated only a moment before she clicked on the email.

Dear Mrs. Williams,

I know you must hate me for what I did to Justin. You're right to. What happened that night was my fault, and I hope you can believe that however much you hate me, it's nothing compared to how much I hate myself for what happened.

I only want you to know I'm sorry. I know I can't ever make it up to you, but I want to help in any way I can. I keep seeing news reports about Justin and every time, I think it should be me. I wish it had been. It isn't fair.

Please, if I can do ANYTHING, let me know.

I know I don't have any right to ask this, but if Justin is okay, if he's recovering, could you tell me? It's hell not to know.

I'm so sorry.

Sincerely,

Tina Castro

Mary stared at the message and fought a lump in her throat while her eyes stung with hot tears. *It isn't fair.*

She was damned right it wasn't fair. It should be Tina in a

hospital bed right now, Tina who might never wake up, her parents who—

Her heart seized at that thought. If it had been, her parents would be at her bedside. They would lie awake at night, afraid to go to sleep because they knew they would see her grave in their nightmares. They would watch her cheeks grow gaunter by the week, and they would rage at the fact that she was so close to them, still breathing but unreachable.

And her parents would never have received the offer Mary and Tad had. They wouldn't have been in the news to catch PIVOT's attention, and they wouldn't even have had the offer of a bribe. They wouldn't be able to give her a dragon for her birthday.

Mary couldn't wish her pain on anyone, and it would be worse for them.

Her breathing slowed. She no longer needed to sit on her hands to keep from typing an angry tirade. She could close the email without wanting to make Tina's pain worse.

But she couldn't find kind words yet. Not yet. She couldn't face the woman who'd taken Justin's life away and exposed Tad to threats of blackmail.

Not yet.

She snatched her purse, powered the computer down, and left for the PIVOT labs.

CHAPTER FIVE

The two young engineers stared at the breakfast burrito on the kitchenette table. It had been thirty minutes since Jacob had arrived with the four burritos and twenty minutes since they had finished theirs. Now, with Amber still not there, both of them began to wonder how dead they would be if they ate hers as well.

DuBois, meanwhile, wandered into the kitchenette with his hand over his sternum. "So heavy," he complained.

"You can't only eat popcorn, man." Jacob gave him a hard look. "I'm…worried about you. And I lived on ramen and vodka for a year."

"Two years," Nick corrected him and said to the other man, "And you should take him seriously. He knows what he's talking about. He got scurvy. Literal scurvy."

The doctor swung to face them, clearly interested in this development. "Really?"

"We don't need to go into this," Jacob said grumpily.

"He didn't work it out for a while," Nick said wickedly, "because when he's sick, he gets himself two cartons of orange juice and drinks them straight. You should have seen his face when he finally put two and two together."

His teammate grumbled and looked up as Amber wandered into the room. She wore the same clothes she had the day before, and the shadows under her eyes were so dark that he had to double-check to make sure she hadn't been in a fight.

"Hi," she said distractedly and made a beeline for the coffee.

"We got you a breakfast burrito," Jacob said.

"Thanks." She drained an entire cup of coffee, wiped a drip off the edge of her mouth, and threw the mug in the trash. "Wait. That doesn't go there." She fished it out and put it in the little dishwasher. "More coffee."

"Did you sleep at all?" Jacob asked her.

"No." She came to sit, cradling a new mug in both hands. When she realized it was empty, she stared at it blankly until Nick stood and retrieved the pot. "Thanks."

"Why were you up?" Nick asked her.

"Uh…"

"She was researching the reporter who got in," DuBois said. "And who she tackled," he added darkly.

"You did what?" Jacob gave her a horrified look. "Wait— someone got in?"

"Yes." Amber gave him a weary look and gulped her coffee. "I didn't hurt her and I didn't confirm that Justin was here, but I spent the night trying to find out who she worked for and also to buy a better security system. The landlord agreed to let us put in whatever we wanted."

"Did he agree to that because you called him at an ungodly time of the morning and he simply wanted to go back to sleep?"

"Possibly." She raised an eyebrow. "Don't judge my method. I get results. I'll need you to scrounge up another ten grand for the system, though."

"Didn't we get five million from our mystery donor?" Nick interjected.

"It goes more quickly than you'd think," Jacob said. "Between the servers and everything else, we don't have much left, especially with trying to stabilize the power fluctuations."

"Oh, we resolved that last night, too." Amber finished her second cup of coffee and Nick poured her another. "I switched a few of the servers to a different block of circuits and also unplugged the most power-hungry machine we had."

"You killed Justin?"

"No, you idiot." She rolled her eyes. "There's one thing in this office that sucks a wildly variant amount of power and was made with zero thought to efficiency, and that's the giant, deluxe popcorn machine."

The two young men looked at DuBois, who regarded the ceiling with sudden, fanatical interest.

"The...the popcorn machine," Jacob said after a fairly tense silence.

"Yep."

"That's why we kept having blackouts."

"Yep."

"Well, selling it will get us some of our security money." He sighed. "It looks like it's back to store-bought popcorn for you, buddy."

The doctor muttered and headed into the lab as Mary entered the kitchenette. She looked almost as distracted as Amber and raised her eyebrows to see all of them.

"I only saw one car in the parking lot."

"Well, DuBois never leaves and Nick and I carpooled," Jacob explained. "But...Amber, where did you park?"

"I took an Uber," she said. "Do you honestly think I should be driving?"

"Good point." He smiled at Mary. "How are you?"

"I'm...not important. Did you say something about security?"

The three members of the PIVOT team looked at one another and tried to reach a silent consensus before Jacob explained. "The press seems to have found out where we are, and we'd like to make sure no one can simply walk in."

"You should call my husband," Mary suggested.

"I really wouldn't want to bother him," he said.

"No, I mean it's possible he could get you funding." She raised an eyebrow. "Senators are always meeting with donors and quite a few have had funding for their pet projects pushed through. Why shouldn't we?"

"Uh…" Unsure what to do with this sudden change in perspective on her part, he gave her a blank smile. "I'll…um, I'll give him a call. Nick, would you like to walk Mrs. Williams through the pod setup?"

"Please call me Mary," the woman said as she moved away with the other engineer. "I feel old enough as it is around you three."

Jacob smiled and followed them but returned a moment later to pull gently on Amber's arm. She shambled along in his wake, still sipping at her coffee and her eyes focused on the middle distance. He wondered idly if she'd notice if he thunked her over the head with a brick.

Not that he'd risk it, of course. In a fight between a sleep-deprived, zombified Amber and anyone up to and including a rabid bear, he'd bet on her every time.

As they had requested, Mary had come dressed in more casual clothes than she usually wore. From what Jacob could tell, she had purchased her sweatpants and long-sleeved t-shirt specifically for this experiment, and she looked—ironically—very uncomfortable when she took her coat off.

"Okay," Nick said. His tone was very soothing and he had realized she was worried. "You remember how the game started for Justin? He was alone and had to hunt rabbits, avoid wolves, and all of that. You won't have to do anything like that, okay?"

The woman nodded. Her arms were wrapped around herself now and she stared at the pod as she shivered nervously.

"When you get into the game world, you'll be in a comfortable room," he continued. "You will see windows that lead to a pleasant seaside view, and there will be sounds like waves and birds singing. You can stay there as long as you want."

Mary looked heartened at that.

"There will be different challenges around the room." He opened the pod and gestured for her to sit, smoothly beginning the preparations as he kept her mind occupied with the details. "Objects to pick up and fit together, a thin carpet on the floor for you to try to walk along, things like that. This will help you get used to the game controls."

Jacob was impressed. The woman was scared—as, he had to admit, he would be if he'd never used this technology before. The only person she had ever seen in this world was locked inside it.

Nick took her hand to help her lie inside the pod, then clipped a pulse monitor on her finger while he attached electrodes to her head. DuBois hovered at the side and watched carefully. He did not intervene, however. The group had decided together that, when it came to Mary, it would be best to have someone with a good bedside manner to introduce the world.

"We've taken your pulse every time you've been in recently," Nick told her, "so we have a good idea of your resting pulse rate. If we sense that you're stressed or uncomfortable, we'll stop the simulation—you'll see the world fade out like a sunset. You can also stop the simulation at any time by saying, 'stop the simulation.' We'll be able to hear your voice, remember, exactly like with Justin."

"Right." She looked at them. Her face was pale. "What will happen if it…doesn't work?"

"It could go wrong in a number of ways," DuBois said. He fell silent when Amber gave him a death glare of epic iciness.

"It boils down to one of two possibilities," she told Mary. The coffee must be kicking in because she looked mostly human by now. "Either you won't be able to get the input and you won't see or hear anything, in which case you can tell us that. Or the game won't take your input, in which case you won't be able to move. We'll be able to see either of those two things happen, so we'll simply stop the simulation and one of us will troubleshoot."

The woman nodded wordlessly.

"Okay," Nick said. "Now, close your eyes and when you open them, you should be in the seaside room and you'll hear my voice."

Mary closed her eyes and he pressed the button to begin the simulation. Her muscles twitched and her eyes began to move behind her closed eyelids. He watched her carefully and examined the vital sign feeds before he closed the lid of the pod.

"Mary, can you hear me?"

"I can hear you." The voice was surprised. "How am I speaking?"

"I'll have Amber show you the mechanism." Nick smiled. "What do you see?"

"I'm in a room like you said. I think it's a castle."

"Describe it in as much detail as you can."

On the screen, the team could see the room she was in—thanks to the recent upgrades the mysterious donation had purchased for them—and Amber was poised to take notes on any differences they saw between her description and reality.

"The stone is gray," Mary said. "There are rugs on the floor. One is an oriental rug, another is a very long, thin rug. They look thick—oh!" The floor rushed up as her character fell. "How do I get up?"

"Relax for a moment," Nick told her. "Breathe. Give me a long breath—in, two, three…hold…out, two, three. Now stand up."

The camera righted itself and she asked, "How did that work?"

"The game responds to your intent and what your body thinks it's doing," he explained. "You sent the nerve impulses to stand, so that's what you did in the game. But it's like juggling or knitting. If you think about it too hard, you can't do it—you have to do it subconsciously."

"Huh." She took a few unsteady steps to the window. "Oh, it's beautiful. You wanted me to describe things, right? I must be high up. I can see the water and the sunlight on it. There are no clouds. Oh, a bird! The water is so lovely, and I hear the waves, even though I don't think I should be able to. There's wind."

"Good, good. Do you smell anything?"

"No."

"That one seems to take longer," Nick said to Amber, who nodded. Justin had also taken a while to smell and taste things in the game, and the feed still wasn't perfect.

"Can you run through some of the tests?" Nick asked her. "Try picking things up and putting them down, stacking them on top of one another, et cetera."

"Okay." Mary walked slowly to the table on one side of the screen, and they watched as she began trying to pick things up. It took her a few attempts to close her fingers around something successfully, and her depth perception was a little off at first.

"Mary, do you wear glasses?"

"When I read," she said. "Oh. *Oh.* I see."

"Yeah." He considered. "I think we might have to work with things as they are for now. I wouldn't be surprised if things adjust over time, but you could have trouble with depth perception when you log in and log out."

They watched her complete the trials, mostly in silence. Amber, at Jacob's urging, left him to take notes and headed off to devour her breakfast burrito. DuBois periodically stared longingly at his now-unplugged popcorn machine. Nick fiddled with the controls.

Finally, Mary picked up one of the objects and, after a pause, threw it out the window of the room. It sailed away and she laughed before she ran to look out. The world tilted dizzily as she gazed at the city below.

"Oh, dear. Oh, I don't like heights."

"That's good to know," Nick told her. "Next time you load in, you'll be on the ground floor."

"Thank you." The view swung crazily as she looked around. "Where did the plate land? I didn't hit anyone, did I?"

"Even if you did, they're not real," DuBois said.

"I still don't want to hurt them."

"That's illogical." The doctor opened his mouth to speak again and received an elbow in the side. "Ow! What was that for?"

"She's being nice," Jacob said. "That's one of the things that'll stave off the robot apocalypse. Don't call it illogical."

DuBois shut up but he looked deeply skeptical.

"Okay, Mary," Nick said, "you can now choose what your character will look like. Three options will pop up in front of you."

In the viewfinder, three magical portals appeared. The first, with a white background, showed a woman with blonde hair caught in a high ponytail and a costume reminiscent of a certain warrior princess but with more cleavage. The second, with a blue background, showed a woman with a wide-brimmed pirate's hat and an eyepatch, her white shirt slightly translucent and thigh-length high-heeled boots over tight pants. She blew a kiss. The third wore a plunging green gown and held a ball of flame in her cupped hands. Her black hair swirled in an imaginary wind.

Mary seemed dumbstruck. No sound came from the monitor. Finally, she said faintly, "Ah...I'm not sure I'm comfortable wearing any of this."

Amber gave Nick one of her trademark Fix-It-Now looks. "I'm sorry, Mary," she said quickly. "These are some of the default characters that were here when we acquired the game. This should have been fixed. One moment." She pressed a few keys to remove the portals and leaned forward to look Nick in the eyes. "This is something I never thought I'd have to say but stop objectifying the senator's wife."

"I'm sorry!" he squeaked. He began typing furiously on another computer. "I loaded the wrong game assets. I swear. Don't kill me. Okay, this should work. One second…" He hesitated and looked genuinely frightened before he pressed a button nervously.

This set of characters, Jacob saw with relief, was much better. The first wore flowing red robes. Her face was in shadow but they could see a hint of grey hair, and black power swirled in one hand. The second wore armor much like Zaara's, although it was brown instead of black, and a deep-red cloak. She was younger but not as heavily made up as the women from the first set. The third had heavier plate armor and wore a sword strapped across her back.

"I like the first one," Mary said. She sounded quite pleased. "I see why Justin likes this so much. I'd love to be able to throw spells at people when I get older—and sweep around in fancy robes like that."

"I can't help you with the spells," Amber said, "but I'm fairly sure the robes are doable."

The woman laughed.

"Okay," Nick said. "I'll walk you through a few trials that should show us how well your buffs are working. If everything is good, I'll port you to Justin's zone, okay? Head to the door."

As they watched Mary emerge improbably into a meadow, DuBois leaned closer to murmur to Amber, "If this works, you have more than merely a recovery tool. You have a way for people to interact with their loved ones while they're in a coma."

Her mouth gaped. She'd been so caught up in tracking their mysterious benefactor that she hadn't thought about the other applications of their research.

"We could even use it for people to speak to loved ones after they die," the doctor continued.

"Shhhh," she hissed.

"Not Justin—anyone. Imagine being able to speak to a parent or a grandparent…or a spouse who'd passed away."

"Holy shit," she murmured. "Uh, Jacob? We'll want that in some marketing materials at some point."

"Wait." DuBois gestured at the screen. "Let's see if it works first."

The engineer buried his face in his hands. "Buzzkill," he said.

CHAPTER SIX

The ruins lay a fair distance from town—easily a day's journey, although they could see the faint shimmer of them nestled in the hollow of a mountain long before they reached them.

As they walked, Zaara and Lyle bickered good-naturedly about the various mythology of the dwarves, so Justin was able to let his mind drift. He could only think it was a shame that he wouldn't have all these hard-earned muscles in reality when he woke.

That thought led him to wonder what it would be like to wake up. Would he come out of sleep all at once, or would he go to sleep one night in the game and wake up in the real world? Would the doctors tell him what they were going to do?

Would he have a chance to say goodbye to people?

When he glanced at his companions, he felt a pang of sadness. He knew they weren't real, but the thought of vanishing out of their lives without so much as a goodbye seemed cruel. Would other people encounter them in the game and hear about Justin, the adventurer who had disappeared?

Lyle saw him looking at them and his brows snapped together.

"Yer lookin' peaky," he told him. "It's that armor. Yer not strong enough for it yet. And ye know why, don't ye?"

"Because this is the first time I've worn it?" He did feel exhausted, now that the dwarf mentioned it, and he thought that was very unfair. After all, he wasn't *really* hauling around a suit of plate armor.

"No. It's because ye don't drink enough ale." The dwarf nodded seriously. "We'll start working on that in the next town we get to."

"Uh…" Justin wondered what his parents would say if he came out of this experience otherwise recovered but suddenly a raging alcoholic.

"Hey, look." Zaara, thankfully, distracted Lyle. "There's a cart up ahead. It looks like it's broken down, though."

The three of them increased their pace and the AI made snide comments now and then as Justin panted and wished vaguely for death. Luckily, they weren't too far from the cart and soon stared at a large man who held a hammer in astonishingly well-muscled forearms.

"Greetings," he said, but his tone wasn't very friendly. Nearby, the horse tied to the cart pranced nervously, and Justin could see that the wheel beside the man's leg had cracked.

"We're on our way to the ruins in the shadow of the mountain," he said, "and I see that your cart is broken. Is there anything we can do to help you fix it?"

The man gave them a measuring glance. "Where'd you come from, then?"

"East Newbrook," Zaara explained. "We've been there for some weeks—well, I have. These two only arrived a week or so ago."

"Aye, what news of the wizard?"

"He's gone," she told him and glanced skyward. "Some of his magic lingers, but he's dead."

"That's what I'd heard." He scratched his chin, now thoughtful. "It's why I decided to come along, see. I'm looking for a job."

"As an adventurer?" Justin asked. "You could come with us. We could always use more weapons and you look like you'd be good with that hammer."

"Ha." The man chuckled. "I have no interest in adventuring. I'll leave that to you. But it seems you aren't highwaymen, so how'd you like to make a few coins?"

He bowed. "We're at your service."

Zaara gave a snort of ill-concealed amusement and his cheeks flushed.

The man, thankfully, pretended not to notice. "A wolf scared my donkey off," he explained. "A great, hulking beast came out of the woods and tried to get the donkey away from me. I had a hell of a time keeping the horse calm—that's how we struck the rock that cracked the wheel—and I managed to scare the wolf off, but the donkey ran as well. I'd appreciate you finding it before the wolf finds itself a nice meal."

"We can do that." Justin stopped himself before he bowed again. "Which direction did the donkey go?"

"Thataway." He pointed. "I hoped he'd come back, but no such luck."

"We'll take a look." He gestured to Zaara. "Ladies first."

"You know, when people say that, I don't think they mean ladies should lead the way into wolf-infested territory." She grinned as she started off. "Also, feel free to stay here. You're struggling in that armor, aren't you?"

"Shut up." He panted as he clanked after her.

The meadows sloped away from the road in a series of winding hills dotted with stands of trees. It would have been quite pretty if not for the fact that he knew he would have to climb the hills when this was over.

He considered taking the armor off, but if he did that, Zaara would laugh again.

Lyle gave a low whistle a few minutes later and stopped to point. The donkey grazed in a patch of open grass, and it looked at them warily as they approached. Zaara, thankfully, must have learned something about farm animals because she approached it from the side and let it sniff her before she slipped a hand around its halter.

"There, now," she told it. "Should we get you back home?"

"Uh…Zaara?" Justin stared at the nearby stand of trees. "Zaara, we have a new friend."

"I know, isn't he sweet?" She stroked the donkey's ears.

"Not the donkey, ye daft lass. Look," Lyle muttered. "Look at the trees."

She complied and her eyes widened when she saw the shadow lurking there. They'd found the donkey barely in time, it seemed, because the wolf that had spooked the cart had arrived.

"There's something wrong with it," Zaara said. She had stepped in front of the donkey and her other hand rested on the hilt of a knife.

"Is the something perhaps that it's twice the size any wolf should be?" he whispered in response. "Lyle, I see you're thinking of charging. Do not."

"It's part of the plan," the dwarf whisper-shouted at him.

"The tank pulls."

"What does that even mean?"

"It means I go first." Justin burst into a run without waiting for a response and immediately regretted his decision. His armor was heavy and fatigue points had him down to three-quarters health without having reached the wolf yet.

The beast didn't run and instead, charged to meet him. He didn't have the nimbleness to dodge anymore, although he tried as best he could. The only result was that he tumbled awkwardly in a heap of clattering armor pieces without changing direction at all, after which the wolf collided with him at high speed.

In the darkened lab, everyone except Nick clapped a hand over their mouth. Even DuBois, perpetually intrigued by the mechanics of the game instead of taking it seriously, looked faintly queasy.

"Oh, dear," he said.

"Ohhhhhhh." Amber shook her head in disbelief. "Oh, no."

"What's going on?" Mary asked. "What do I hear in the background?"

"I, uh—I knocked the coffee machine over," Amber told her and motioned to everyone else to be quiet. To the others, more quietly, she added, "I hope he learns about the sword soon. It won't help him if he never gets a chance to swing it."

REALLY BAD TANK, LEVEL 3

The wolf seemed as surprised to be bulldozed by Justin as he was by falling instead of dodging. As much as anything that was four hundred pounds of killing machine could trip, it did and skidded while it scrabbled to get its feet under it again.

"Stooooooooout!"

"Goddammit…" he muttered as he tried to roll over.

"You know, when I had them belabor the idea of you being a tank, I didn't think you'd be quite this bad at it."

"Oh, so you weren't trying to get me killed? That's reassuring." He glared at the sky.

"You always look up when you talk to me. I'm not God, you know. I'm an AI."

"Whatever." He managed to haul himself up and leaned

heavily on his sword as he glowered at Lyle, who dodged wildly around the wolf. It wasn't quite sure what to do with a short force of nature, but once in a while, it would stretch its neck and snap its teeth to force him to dance away.

"Justin!" the dwarf panted. "The sooner you can get up, the better. My fists are doing nothing."

"Almost like punching a wolf was a flawed concept," Justin retorted as he took a step and slashed with all his might at one of the wolf's hind legs.

The effect was unexpectedly good. Fifty hit points floated away and took a chunk of the wolf's health bar with it. The creature stumbled heavily to the side. It whipped its head around with a snarl and he resisted the urge to run away. He was a tank and needed to stand his ground.

At least he'd captured its attention.

"Zaara! Hit it with everything you have."

"I'm on it!" she yelled as he planted his feet and swung his weapon. It was much harder, he discovered, to stand his ground when he was in a virtual reality. Like most people he knew, he had laughed at the videos of people in VR games who cowered and screamed while being attacked.

It turned out that your nervous system was a hell of a lot stronger than your tactical brain. He didn't curl into a ball on the ground but he hunched his shoulders, planted his feet, and held the sword out. Again, the blade sliced cleanly through fur and flesh and again, a chunk of hit points came away. Although he was thrown back several feet and ended up on his butt in the dirt, the impact didn't do as much damage as he'd expected.

Score one for the armor.

REALLY BAD TANK, LEVEL 4

"Oh, come on!" Justin yelled at the sky. "Zaara? Any minute now."

"I'm trying," she responded. "I've thrown three fireballs and they don't do anything."

"Wait, what?" Justin scrambled back as the wolf advanced. It was limping but it had murder in its eyes. The beast snapped at him once, looked at the other two, and seemed to be trying to decide what to do.

Apparently, he would have to be the one to end this. He came to a quick decision and slumped in the dirt.

"Justin!" Zaara yelled.

The wolf seized its chance and leapt.

Its weight and momentum carried it forward powerfully and into three feet of steel that pierced its belly. Justin threw his head and torso sideways as the huge body slumped onto the sword and he felt a wrenching pain in his elbow. He released the weapon with a yell and curled into a ball as he tried to push himself up on his good arm. The other wasn't dislocated, he was sure, but his nervous system sure thought it should be.

This was worse than the widow's salve. Dear God. He hobbled to the wolf's side, grasped the sword, and made to yank it out but stared as the beast shrank and faded away before his eyes. On the ground lay a bloodied, bruised man who stretched toward him.

"You have to—help them—" He gasped as he tried to speak.

"What?" Justin stared at him in horror. He hadn't felt sad to kill the zombies around Sephith's tower—they were already dead, after all—and he hadn't felt sad to kill Sephith, who manifestly deserved it. But this man was scared and now, he recalled that the wolf had only charged him once he attacked.

He hadn't behaved like a wolf because he wasn't one. Justin knelt at his side as Zaara ran closer with the bag of salves.

"Lie still," she told the man.

"No." He shook his head. "Too—late. You have to listen." His hand closed around Justin's. "There are more of us. Not werewolves. Witch…cursed us. We robbed her and she cursed us. You have to help."

"You robbed a woman and now you're preying on livestock," Zaara said, offended. "And you want us to help you?"

"Only—trying to survive," the man rasped. "A wolf still has to eat. Kill her and the spell will release them. Then…justice." He looked like he wanted to say more but before he could, he slumped in the dirt and lay still.

Justin's stomach heaved. He hadn't ever seen anyone die before, and although this wasn't the real world, it felt real. The smell of blood hung in the air and the man had talked to him moments before going still. He had felt the way his sword sliced through his flesh and with something close to horror, realized he was the reason for the body in the dirt.

To his surprise, it was Lyle who seemed to understand. The dwarf came to lay a heavy hand on his shoulder. "It shouldn't get easier t'kill men," he advised him. "When I left for a life aboveground, that's what my da told me. He said to do whatever I wished but when it got easier to kill a man, I'd know it was time to seek another life." He held a hand out and hauled him to his feet. "Let's bring this donkey back and rest, eh?"

CHAPTER SEVEN

W alking the donkey to its owner was a silent affair. Zaara seemed unsure of what to say, and Lyle had spoken his piece already and didn't seem inclined to add to it.

Justin, meanwhile, did his best to not feel like he'd made a terrible mistake. Zaara's suggestion of holing up in a tavern seemed like a better and better idea with each passing moment. It was one thing to go after a megalomaniac with a horde of zombie servants, but this kind of thing made him sick to his stomach.

"Only trying to survive," the man had said.

The donkey's owner studied them critically when they arrived. "What in the seven hells happened to you?"

"We found the wolf," he said shortly.

The man gave him a long look. "Well, I think I'll camp for the night," he said at last. "You're welcome to share my fire. I don't have much coin for you as a thanks, but I'll say this. I'm a black-smith, and a good one. When next you're in East Newbrook, I'll add touches to that armor of yours, sharpen your swords and knives, whatever you need. You, dwarf—I can sharpen those talons with what I have here."

The blacksmith gathered rocks for a fire with Lyle, who

seemed to explain the fight in a low tone. Zaara took one look at Justin's face, wisely decided not to talk to him, and let him wander away from the camp.

He stripped his armor off and wrapped one of the blankets from his pack over his shirt. As the others set up camp, made dinner, and finished the wagon repairs, he prowled the outskirts. The first stars began to twinkle on the eastern horizon when he saw the woman emerge from the shadows.

She wore flowing robes and she walked confidently toward him.

The hair on his arms stood up. No one should be out there at twilight alone, and especially not without a weapon. More than that, though, she seemed familiar in a way he couldn't put his finger on.

"Are you fucking with me?" he asked the AI under his breath.

"*I am not.*" Unfortunately, it volunteered no more information.

The woman moved closer and stared at him for a long time. When she pulled her hood back, white hair gleamed in the light of the rising moon. Her face wore an expression that he couldn't name.

"Justin?" she asked, and her voice cracked.

He took a step back. "Are you the witch?" Please, let someone at the camp see him. Why had he walked away from his sword?

To his surprise, she smiled and he saw a tear trace down one cheek. She gave a laugh that sounded a little like a sob. "I'm not a witch but you have called me that once or twice. Justin...it's me. It's Mom."

"Mom?" His voice came out louder than he wanted it to. In the camp, there was a sudden scuffle of activity and in moments, Lyle and Zaara were there. He looked at them and shook his head. "Could I, uh—could I have a moment with her? Thanks."

They retreated but he saw Lyle sink into the shadows near one of the cartwheels to keep watch on the two of them.

Justin turned to the woman. "You're...you're really Mom? No

offense, but this whole virtual world scenario is playing with my head. Can you prove it?"

"Yes." She smiled again, although she still looked like she wanted to cry. "When you were seven, you broke your arm falling off the rope swing at Joey Thaler's house. I wrapped you in the green quilt Grandma made you and we brought you to the hospital in Dad's old truck."

"Mom." He took two steps and embraced her so tightly she squeaked. "Sorry. I didn't mean to—oh, no." His heart dropped. "Oh, no. Mom. Are you okay? Why are you here?"

"I'm okay!" She clasped his hands. "I came to see you. I wanted to spend time with my boy."

Despite being twenty-four, he had the distinct urge to stomp his foot and remind her that he wasn't a little kid anymore.

"Moooooooom, I'm a dragon slayer!"

He wished hellfire and missed server connections on the AI but held his tongue rather than respond to the sniped comment. To his mother, he said quietly, "How long has it been?"

"A month and a half," she said at once with the recall of someone who had thought of almost nothing else. "They say it's only been a week and a half or so for you in here."

Justin swallowed. "Is that…good? Or bad?"

"I asked. DuBois said it simply is." His mother sounded frustrated and she shook her head. "He said these things take time and your brain needs to rest. There are good signs."

He looked at the camp. The fire crackled and the smell of food cooking drifted on the air. His stomach growled and his muscles ached. It seemed incredible that this wasn't a real place. He debated saying something about how he'd miss it but decided not to. He knew his mother wouldn't understand that.

"How's Dad?" he asked instead.

A series of expressions crossed her face too quickly to track. "He's fine," she said.

"Really?" he pressed.

She took her time to choose her words. "It doesn't take lobbyists very long to discover what motivates you. They tried money and it didn't work. Now, they're trying blackmail."

"Blackmail?"

His mother wavered, then shrugged dismissively. "They doctored photos of him to make it seem like he was having an affair. And, yes, I know they did because I remember that day—I was the one who was with him. He liked to think it wouldn't be complicated when he got to the senate and that he'd always know what to do, but he's finding out it's…not that easy."

Justin nodded.

"He's worried about you," Mary said quietly. "He flies out on the red-eye for his sessions and comes back at night. Every night, he's here and he comes to see you."

He looked away and a lump formed in his throat. "Can we… talk about something else?"

"Of course." She reached for his hand. "How are you?"

"Not that, either." He gave a watery laugh and remembered something. "Where's Tina? Why isn't she here with me?" When he saw the look on his mother's face, he had to take a moment to process it. It wasn't sadness, he realized. It was anger.

It was fury, in fact.

"Tina," his mother said, "is fine."

"Oh, thank God." He pressed a hand over his heart.

"Thank God?" His mother's voice rose. "She crashed that car at ninety miles per hour. You've been in a coma for weeks now, Justin, while she walked away with scratches. And you say thank God?"

"I don't want her dead," Justin said. He frowned at her. "It isn't like you to want someone hurt either."

"I never had someone crash a car with my son in it before," Mary said fiercely. She squeezed his fingers. "It isn't fair. She's the one who messed up and you're the one to pay the price—and, Justin, it's my fault, too. I made you go on that date. If I'd let you stay home like you wanted to that night, you'd be safe now." She pressed a hand over her mouth.

"Mom—"

"No, no. Don't you comfort me. You're the one who's hurt. I came to comfort you." She forced herself to smile.

"Mom." He took her hands. "Don't blame yourself and don't blame Tina. It was an accident. A puppy ran into the road and she didn't want to hit it. This was an accident. It isn't worth hating her over and it isn't like you to do that."

She sighed and nodded but didn't meet his gaze.

"Mom." The word came out before he knew he was speaking. "Will I be okay?"

The way her gaze snapped to his face, he knew she didn't know. On some level, that was comforting—he'd been afraid, he realized, that she was there because she knew he would never get better.

"There's progress," she told him. "Your brain function is improving. They say it's sustained, not merely a fluke."

"Okay." He nodded, dizzy with relief.

"Oh, I've missed you." His mother wrapped him in her arms. "I've missed you so much, Justin."

"I've missed you," he whispered in return. He slid his arms around her back and squeezed until his arms closed on nothing. His mother's face shimmered in the air, blurred out of focus into pixels, and vanished.

For a long moment, he stood and stared at the space where she'd been.

"That's yer mother?" Lyle said from behind him. "She's not the witch, is she?"

Justin laughed. He needed to laugh right now and he was absurdly grateful for the dwarf's presence. "She's not the witch," he said. "She's, ah…you know, it's one of those long stories that aren't as good as the Buttercup one. But if you want, I can tell you all about Luke Skywalker."

CHAPTER EIGHT

Her arms closed around thin air and Justin disappeared like a ghost. Mary opened her mouth to scream as everything around her faded into deep blue studded with stars, then disappeared entirely.

"Justin! DuBois!"

Cold air rushed over her and hands touched her forehead and wrists. The first thing she saw when she opened her eyes was a flood of light. DuBois and Nick removed the patches from her head, their faces strained and pale.

"What happened?" Mary demanded. "Is he okay?"

"He's fine," the young engineer said tightly.

"Well, am I fine? My pulse wasn't rising, I wasn't panicked—"

"It wasn't that." Nick glanced over her shoulder.

"What, then?" She looked at DuBois, who now stood with his shoulders hunched. He didn't meet her gaze as she slid off the table. "Well? So help me, but if you tell me again that I can't see Justin because—"

"Mrs. Williams." Amber's voice was impressively level. Far too level, in fact. "We were instructed to pull you out of the game."

Mary turned slowly. She had the feeling she wouldn't like

what she saw and she was right. Two men in suits stood near Amber and Jacob, along with four in bulletproof vests. Jacob was in handcuffs.

She used the same tone she'd used when she came into the house to find Justin setting his winter coat on fire using one of the stove burners. "What is going on here?"

"Ma'am, I'm Agent Klein from the Food and Drug Administration." One of the men stepped forward. "I regret to inform you that there is no FDA approval for this human testing, nor has approval been sought. The lab needs to be shut down."

"Shut down—no." Mary drew herself tall. "No. You can't do that." A part of her registered the oddness of the situation because it somehow felt like a few steps had been omitted from the entire process. It didn't add up, but her brain couldn't think it through.

"They can, Mrs. Williams." Amber shook slightly as she spoke. Her hands were clenched at her sides and wrinkled the sheaf of papers she held in one hand. "We have twenty-four hours to shut the lab down and Jacob is…" She looked at her teammate and swallowed.

"As the President of PIVOT Technologies, I am legally responsible for what happened here," Jacob said. He cleared his throat. "As well as ethically responsible, Mrs. Williams. I hope you won't hold Dr. DuBois, Amber, or Nick responsible for this. I led them to believe we had received FDA approval."

Mary realized what he was doing at the same time Amber did. Their jaws dropped.

"I truly am sorry, Mrs. Williams." He looked miserable and she decided he didn't need to fake that, not with jail time looming. "I had seen the research and the early results were so good, I was sure this was a good way to help Justin. But—"

"That's enough, Mr. Zachary." One of the agents stepped in front of him. "Mrs. Williams, our office will be in contact with you. Ms. Garcia, Mr. Ryan, Dr. DuBois—this lab is to be shut down within twenty-four hours. We will send an agent to oversee the process. Mrs. Williams, you will need to arrange for your son's transfer to an approved medical facility." He gave the team a cold look before he gestured to Jacob. "Mr. Zachary, come with us, please."

The officials left and the young engineers watched their friend go with horrified faces. When they were alone, Amber turned and Mary stepped forward, her chin trembling.

"You let them take him? You're letting them do this?"

Amber held the pieces of paper out. "They have the authority, it seems. The FDA has blanket authority over all drug trials except in very specific instances."

"This is the only thing that's keeping Justin alive!" Her voice was raw. She turned away, a hand over her mouth. "If they take him off this, he'll be locked in, he'll be alone—" She broke off and stared at the wall. "We knew the risks. All of us knew the risks. And they'll haul Jacob up for it and you'll let them?"

"No." The young woman's voice was firm. "Believe me, we will find a way out of this for Jacob. We have legal representation and Nick is calling them now. They'll meet him at the police station, and he knows not to say anything until a lawyer is present. Beyond that..." She faltered for a moment before her voice strengthened. "Beyond that, I'm not sure what to do, but we'll think of something. Keeping Justin on this treatment is the best way to allow him to heal. The first problem—aside from the fact that the FDA might have overstepped—is the time limit the so-called official documentation stipulates. What we need to find is...somewhere to take him where they let us keep doing this on the sly?" She shook her head. "But the agents will check when he's installed."

Mary watched her and her anger drained slowly. "You'll be arrested, too."

Amber gave her a sharp look. "Only if we get caught," she said simply.

"There are good odds of that," she insisted. She wanted so badly to agree and send Justin to another facility and make the FDA find them again—anything for a few more days. Every second they delayed was another second in which Justin might wake up. At the same time, she knew what they were risking, and the mother in her didn't want the other woman to spend her life in jail for this. She looked at Nick and Amber. "You two may face jail time if you help us now. You know that."

"That's now how I'm making my decision," Amber said.

Mary sighed.

The friends exchanged a look.

"What?" Nick asked.

"Well," Mary said and looked around for her purse, "I can't let you all go to jail for trying to help my son. I'll call Tad. It's time to pull all the strings we can."

"No," Tad heard one of his assistants say. "The Senator is not taking interviews about his son at this time."

"—official press release from our office forty minutes ago," another man said.

A third voice cut over the other two. "—comment on that at this time—"

Tad cradled his head in his hands and groaned. He had tried to spend this morning getting some reading done. The simple truth was that he hated being away from Justin at all, which meant he needed to make every second count when he was there. With the phones ringing off the hook, however, not only was he unable to focus, his staffers couldn't get any of their work done either.

The question from the reporter had set off a furor. Reporters called at every hour of the day and night, his staff had mentioned being tailed to their homes, and deals he'd been in the process of making had begun to fall through.

Somewhere, he realized bitterly, Metcalfe was sitting back and laughing. He had dared him to do whatever he intended to do, and the man had.

His phone rang and his blood pressure spiked. He snatched the handset without looking and snapped, "For the last time, there will be no press access until otherwise stated."

"Tad, it's me." Mary's voice was tight.

"Oh, God." He squeezed his eyes shut. "I should have known. I'm so sorry. The phones are going off the hook I'm going to have to shut them off and—"

"Tad, we don't have time."

"What?" Mary was rarely this brusque. If she was, it meant something bad. "Is Justin okay?"

"For now." She tried very hard to stay calm and he could hear it in her voice. "But someone alerted the FDA to the PIVOT lab and we've been given twenty-four hours to shut everything down."

"What?" Tad lurched out of his seat. A scuffling sound outside followed immediately and one of his aides stood at the door, his earpiece still on.

"Sir?"

"I'm…it's okay." He held a hand out. "I'll, uh—it's okay."

The man backed out, his eyes wary, and Tad fought a wave of despair. Working for him was turning into political suicide for these staffers. He wasn't only ruining his career, he was ruining theirs too. He slumped into his chair and rubbed his forehead.

"It's Metcalfe," he said.

"Yes," Mary agreed. "The problem is, everything the FDA is doing is legal—apparently, although there might be a few procedural loopholes we can raise—and one of the PIVOT team has been arrested. Jacob," she added as if she'd sensed his question.

"Arrested." The bottom of his stomach dropped.

"Tad, that isn't all."

"It isn't?"

"The other three seem determined to keep the experiment going." Her voice began to tremble. "I don't want to move Justin to a hospital. I can't bear the thought of him being locked away in the dark again—" She broke off.

"Mary, listen to me. Justin knows we're here for him." His focus zeroed in on his wife. She was three thousand miles away and all he wanted to do was fold her in his arms. "And he's a fighter. No matter what, it'll be okay."

"Maybe. But what about for them?" Her voice still trembled. "They're talking about how they want to keep this going because it's his best chance, and I want them to, Tad. I want it more than anything, but I can't let four people spend their entire lives in jail because of us. I can't ask them to do that."

Tad looked at his desk, swallowing hard.

"Is there anything you can do?" Mary whispered. "I don't know—something you can add to a bill, an exception you can get passed. We're not asking for anything bad. This project should have FDA clearance. It should have been cleared years ago. It wasn't blocked because it was dangerous. There has to be an appeal we can put through or—I don't know."

"I think there's something," he said. "I'll, uh—I'll check it out and get back to you."

"Oh, thank God." She was smiling, he could tell from her voice. "I'll let you do that. Thank you, love."

"Of course." His lips were numb. "I love you."

With a heavy sigh, he set the phone down and stared at the wall. His heart was racing now and he couldn't seem to catch his breath.

There was, of course, something he could do to make this stop. He could do one simple thing and all these problems would go away.

He could cave.

When he'd first come to Washington, his purpose had been to challenge lobbyists like Metcalfe. In his fantasies, he would stand tall and lead the way, the news would leak that they had tried to put pressure on him, and he would be hailed as a hero. Following his example, dozens of other senators would come forward. Slowly, the tide would turn away from the lobbyists, and senators would begin to represent their constituents' best interests again.

It hadn't gone that way.

Tad had spun a pencil in his fingers and now, he held it so tightly that it creaked. He put it down hastily before he broke it. Somehow, he needed to find a solution. Surely there was a way out of this.

Except there wasn't. What had Metcalfe said? Oh, right—*you're not the first senator who's come here determined to fight us.* They had won every other time, why not now?

"Sir?" Eddie had returned and held a note out. "A courier arrived with this."

"Is it laced with something?" he asked bitterly. When he saw the look on the young man's face, he regretted the joke. "Sorry, Eddie. I'm very sure it's not laced with anything. Thank you for bringing it in. Also...shut the phones down. Re-record the answering service with the message the legal team advised. You all need a rest."

"Sir." He nodded and handed him the letter before he withdrew.

Ted's name was written on the front of the letter in a scrawl that looked like a doctor's handwriting. There was no postmark. He sighed as he opened it to reveal a single sheet of paper with two lines of text. The first was a phone number and the second read, in handwritten letters, *I can help.*

He looked at the letter. This was Metcalfe. It could only be Metcalfe.

Well, hell, he needed to speak to the man anyway. He snatched the phone, dialed the number, and sat on the table while it rang.

"Diatek Industries," a female voice said. "Office of Anna Price. How can I help you?"

Startled, he made no response.

"Hello?" the woman said cautiously.

"Ah, hello." He cleared his throat. "I received a letter that asked me to call. My name is Tad Williams."

"Ah, Senator." The woman's tone brightened. "Ms. Price is expecting your call. I'll put you through, one moment."

"I—" He stopped when hold music began. Holding the phone between his shoulder and his ear, he slid into his chair and typed *Diatek Industries* into his browser's search bar. The computer was still thinking when the hold music stopped and a new voice spoke.

"Hello, Senator."

"Hello." He leaned in his chair. "You are…Anna Price, your secretary said?"

"Yes. I'd like to speak to you." This woman was brisk. "However, not over the phone. Can you meet?"

"I…yes."

"If you leave now, there will be a flight for you out of the private terminal," Anna said promptly.

"To where, exactly?"

"New York City. I'll see you soon, Senator."

She hung up and Tad stared at the handset as he put it in its cradle. His mind warred with rampant thoughts of rage, suspicion, desperation, and fear. Diatek Industries? He'd never heard of them, and the odds were beyond good that this was another player with Metcalfe's objectives. There was no way in hell he would have ever considered taking a flight like this to only God knew what waited on the other side. Then again, he'd never been quite this desperate before.

On the other hand, he had a certain grim desire not to work

with Metcalfe and those he represented and he was intrigued that the CEO of Diatek—the website had loaded now—had spoken to him directly, not hired a sleazeball to conduct negotiations or turn the screws.

He pushed the negative emotions aside, stood decisively, and retrieved his briefcase and coat before he stepped into the main office.

"I'll need you to cancel all my meetings for the rest of the day," he told the aides. "I'm flying to New York. Eddie, could you call me a car? Sylvia, I'd like you to research Diatek Industries. Find me the names of any senators they've spoken to recently and any bills they've weighed in on one way or another. Forward all of that to my email. I need it before I land."

"I...yes." She nodded.

"I'll be back when I can." He spun on his heel and left before he could say anything he'd regret.

Such as the fact that they really should find other jobs before association with him turned them into pariahs.

CHAPTER NINE

Justin slept fitfully. He woke constantly with a start, hoping he would see his mother return, but he had no such luck. While he couldn't help but be worried by the way she had disappeared, he told himself the game was still running so the issues surely couldn't be that bad.

Toward dawn, he walked a short distance away from the camp and recorded a brief message. "Mom, Dad—it was good to see Mom yesterday. I hope you're both well, and I also hope to see you both soon, in here or out there. Let me know if anything is wrong, I'm worried after Mom disappeared so quickly. I promise I'm well here. I love you." He shut the recorder off before he could start babbling.

Their breakfast with the blacksmith was a hasty meal of leftover flatbread and meat from the night before, and the three of them then watched the cart trundle away. The donkey clomped along behind, now docile.

"Well," he said finally, "I guess we should head to the ruins."

He swore that not a single word would disturb his thoughts, but Zaara and Lyle swung into a well-concerted effort to cheer him up. The banter flowed, jokes both good and bad were exchanged, and despite himself, he began to laugh at a song about a young dwarf stuck in a mine and the bargains he struck with the rock spirits to get out.

The change in the landscape around them was gradual. The rolling plains gave way to forests until the trees were packed so tightly that full sunlight reached the road only rarely. Acorns and leaves crunched underfoot. Birds chirped, squirrels skittered over the branches, and deer and foxes could sometimes be seen in clearings.

After a while, it changed again but wasn't noticeable at first. Every tree had dead branches, after all. There were always fallen leaves, and it wasn't uncommon to see the corpse of a small mammal. No matter how idyllic the surroundings, a forest had both life and death.

The death, however, began to grow stronger. Bare branches became more prevalent. The patches of shadow on the road vanished, but neither the blue sky nor the sunlight seemed particularly warm. Ahead of them, the ruins loomed large and they could now see that the dirt there was as gray as ash.

Gradually, his companions stopped joking and their heads turned at every crack of a branch. They still saw deer but the animals seemed gaunter now. At some point, the birdsong had stopped. Even the blue of the sky seemed faded.

"I don't like this," Zaara said finally. "Ruins are fine. I don't mind ruins. But this? It looks like what my father described right after Sephith defeated Kural. This isn't from a fire. It's not dark enough, and even sickness in plants doesn't kill everything."

Indeed, there was not a living thing in sight. Trees had toppled yet did not seem to be rotting. Bushes stood sparse and prickly. Leaves coated the ground, settled over time but not eaten away by animals or fungus. On the other side of the road, some areas seemed dank and swamp-like, although the expected decay usually found in moist, water-logged areas was absent.

"Nothing is rotting," Justin said slowly. "It's like the cycle stopped at death without going on to new life."

His words sounded unnaturally loud in the stillness but less so than Lyle's snort.

"What are you, a poet? Come on, lad, the place is cursed. Let's leave it at that."

He threw his hands up and caught Zaara's good-natured grin. She jerked her head at the dwarf and shrugged, and he could only nod. Besides that, it helped to have someone to keep him from getting too philosophical about all this. He continued to trudge forward and tried to emulate Lyle's wary acceptance of the place, but she stopped them both.

She didn't speak. The location seemed to discourage speaking. Instead, she gestured to where a little shack had almost fallen apart with age. It leaned precariously, the wood so weathered that its colors merged with the gray and brown forest.

Justin pointed at the shack, then at their packs. For all they knew, there might be supplies in there. In the real world, a place like this wouldn't have a mysterious sword or a helm with plus-five strength, but video games were not the real world.

The other two nodded and they inched off the road. He had many half-memories of stories where you weren't supposed to leave the road under any circumstances, but a few glances over his shoulder showed it remained where it had been. It didn't seem to be vanishing like a mirage, nor did the forest seem to close up around them.

The little house looked like it might have been a storage shed at one point, although he wasn't quite sure why one would build one in the middle of a swamp. Perhaps it was for fish, he thought. Still, there was no chimney and nothing except the four walls and the roof, all leaning on the unstable ground. The door had creaked off its hinges as the building slid and now stood ajar.

He held a hand out to indicate to his friends to wait as he pried the door open. Common sense suggested he make sure it wasn't the only thing holding the building up, so he waited a few seconds to see if there were any ominous creaks. There weren't, so he shrugged and stepped inside.

It took his eyes a moment to adjust but he made out several objects in the darkness. This would be a place to restock, he thought in excitement. There was a table, a mortar and pestle, a stool, a broom—

And a woman. She muttered a single word, rough against his ears, and blinding light burst into his eyes. He staggered back as she uttered a second word and froze the three of them where they stood.

"Justin?" Lyle called. "Zaara?"

"I'm here," Zaara responded. "Damned light. What is this?"

"There's a witch," he told her wearily.

The woman laughed. He couldn't see her, not with the light still blazing, but she could have been any age judging by those muttered words and her laugh. "A witch. A good enough assessment, I suppose. And you three are those who slew Sephith, which means I have a task for you."

"Oh?" Justin raised an eyebrow. He was able to move his face, it seemed, but none of the rest of him. Fortunately, given the fact that he'd been in the middle of a step, the spell also seemed to be holding him up. Still, every muscle strained uselessly to avoid falling.

"I'd wager you'll have heard about the wolves," the witch said. "In fact, I'd wager you've fought one or two. You have that smell."

This was the witch the werewolf had mentioned. The realization flashed through Justin's mind and it must have shown on his face.

"Ah, so you did. And you spoke to one, I assume."

"They told us to free them from the spell," he said. "They're hunting livestock because they have no choice. They don't know how to be wolves. They asked us to kill you."

"Well, I wouldn't advise that," she said simply. "You won't succeed. It would be stupid to try, as you can plainly see."

"So will you turn us into werewolves, too?" Zaara panted and it sounded as if she tried to wrench herself free of the spell.

"No. And don't strain yourself trying to undo the spell, girl. I can see what you're using, and nothing you know will free you from this." The woman muttered another harsh word and the light dimmed. To Justin's surprise, seeing her did not make her age any clearer. She wore robes that obscured her hair, and her face was not young but not old either. Her expression emotionless, she studied them for a moment. "I am glad you came to me. Tracking you was…surprisingly difficult."

Justin had some theories about that and decided to keep them to himself.

"I hope we don't have to remain enemies," the witch said pleasantly.

He snorted before he could help himself. Although he couldn't see Zaara, he could hear that she'd made a similar noise.

"You've trapped us," he pointed out.

"Indeed I have. You'll find it's wise to take precautions when three well-armed individuals stumble into your house without warning." She pulled the stool out and sat. With her fingers laced around her knees, she could be any woman sitting in the sun on a nice day.

Except, of course, that she had them all captive and was apparently responsible for wreaking havoc all across this forest.

"Besides," she pointed out, "you've already taken a job to kill me."

"We haven't taken a job," Zaara said, precisely. "We heard the plea of a dying man who was spelled as a wolf."

"A dying bandit," the witch corrected. "He and his pack would have taken everything I had and probably killed me into the bargain, so I won't trouble my conscience over their fate. Now, I would like you to do a favor for me. I would like you to kill the werewolves."

Justin's stomach twisted. He could only move his head but he made full use of that. His head shook emphatically. "No. I refuse."

"You see the forest around this place," the woman told them. "The wolves are poisoning it. Their very essence is turning the place sickly. Parts are already a swamp."

"So why'd ye make them?" Lyle asked.

She did not answer and merely looked at all three of them in turn. "Will you help?"

"I won't hunt a whole pack of them and kill them," he said. "I don't...hunt humans." He remembered the dying man on the ground. "I killed Sephith for a reason. Being a bandit isn't a good enough reason."

"Oh?" Their captor extended one hand casually and where there had been nothing, a key now glittered with a triangular handle, almost identical to the key Sephith had waved in front of the group only two weeks earlier. "Perhaps this will shift the equation. I had hoped you would aid me for the sake of the forest and that this would be an unexpected reward. But if you will not do that, perhaps seeing your true reward now will help to change your mind."

Justin's breath caught.

"Ah." She had seen the change. "Very interesting. I suspected this was what you were searching for, and it seems I was right. Do we have ourselves a deal, adventurers? You do this one thing —for me, and for the forest—and in return, you get this key, which you so clearly want." Her eyes were very bright and very watchful. "You don't want it for the coin, I can see that much. So why? Are you three secretly scholars? The girl, I could see. But you two?"

Justin said nothing. He had a hunch only, and nothing more.

"I guess I shall see if it is incentive enough." She shrugged. "I should teach you a spell. It will aid you on your quest."

"You're teaching us spells?" Justin asked incredulously. "What's to stop us from coming back to kill you?"

The witch looked at the three of them, all frozen in midair.

"Okay, good point," he said.

SLOW ON THE UPTAKE, Level 1, the game told him.

"What, I didn't get any levels from the tank business?"

"Ah, a self burn. Those are rare."

The woman paid no attention to Justin's muttered words. She moved her hand slightly and the spell relaxed enough to allow him and the others to stand upright. She placed a plain wooden bowl on the ground and she looked hard at all three of them.

"You two—you have magic. Pay attention. Look at the bowl and imagine, in your mind's eye, something being revealed. It could be anything—light falling across a room, a covering drawn away from a statue, the lid rising from a box. Imagine it and let your magic twist in with the imagining."

So she was serious about teaching them spells. Justin stared at the bowl until his eyes crossed. He thought of cutting box lids open, pulling covers off furniture, and of everything he could until he groaned in frustration. He finally gave up but, out of nowhere, an apple appeared in the bowl.

"Did I do it?"

"No." Their captor pointed. "She did."

"I did it!" Zaara sounded incredulous. "I thought of a candle in a dark room and…there it was."

"Good. Now, practice." The witch snapped her fingers and the rest of the spell relaxed. "All of you, go now. You, boy, keep thinking of different ways to visualize. I promise you, there are many things in those ruins to see if you get it right. Go now." She watched them as they approached the door warily. Her head was tilted to the side. "You know, I'm interested to see if you come back."

CHAPTER TEN

They were barely outside the shack before Lyle announced, "We shouldn't trust 'er."

"Shhh," Justin hissed.

"What, ye think she doesn't know how ye feel?" The dwarf gave him a scornful look. "No one who strings people up can think they're well-liked. Plus, she's too clean."

"I'm clean," Zaara protested.

"Who said I trusted you?" He gave her a look but grinned after a moment. "Nah, I've forgiven you for that."

"You've forgiven me for…not smelling…" She sounded like she couldn't believe her ears. With a frown, she looked at Justin, who shrugged.

"Yeah. Yer handy with a blade." Lyle seemed oblivious to the absurdity. "Anyway, I say we don't trust her and we don't trust those wolves, neither."

"Now, hang on." He tripped over a bush and barely saved himself from an ignominious fall in the mud. His stamina was increasing, thankfully faster than it would in real life, but he still wasn't entirely used to the weight. "I thought you'd chosen a side."

"Common sense, lad." Lyle chewed meditatively on a stalk of grass. "When two sides are pointin' fingers, it's wisest not to trust either of 'em."

"I suppose that makes—wait, are you chewing on something you found in a swamp?" Justin felt slightly queasy. "That's terrifying."

"What's wrong with that?"

"What's wrong with—ohhhh, I can't." He struggled up the bank and onto the road. "Finally. I hate mud. I hate it, I hate it, I hate it. Not to mention that it looks stupid on plate armor."

"That's what looks stupid?" Zaara asked. When he gave her a sharp look, she raised an eyebrow. "You don't exactly look like a berserker."

"I'm not a berserker, I'm a…knight."

"When were you knighted?"

"Not literally."

"That makes no sense." She rolled her eyes. "But, to return to the matter at hand, I think Lyle has a good point. We need more information. Also, we need dinner."

"I'm on it." He drew his sword, turned, and slashed at a rabbit.

BUNNY SLAYER, Level 4!

"Hey, I'm getting better at that."

"You used a four hundred damage ultimate on a level-two bunny."

"I like my food dead, what can I say?" He clanked stiffly to the other side of the road where he'd seen several other rabbits take shelter in the tufts of grass.

A few deadly swipes later, the group had a set of rabbits for the next few nights' worth of dinner. Lyle began to skin them while Justin made sure to look away and Zaara made another drying rack.

Justin climbed the tumbled remains of a stone wall. He could almost forget he was in a game when he did anything like this. As things progressed and he became more attuned to the signals the game sent, he could feel the stones under his feet and the shift of the rocks when he stepped.

Either that or this was all his imagination. The thought was sobering. What if the game was only the most basic polygons and he simply built up more and more of it in his head? Worse, what if the game had truly crashed when his mother disappeared and everything since then had been a fever-dream constructed by a brain that was locked in the dark?

And how did he know his mother had been there at all? Sure, she knew about him falling and breaking his arm, but he knew about that, too.

He stopped and stared at nothing.

"Justin?" Zaara studied him carefully, a branch held in one hand and a knife in the other. "Are you sick? Do you…see something? Oh, are you practicing the spell?"

"I'm—yes. Yes, that's what I'm doing." He forced a smile. Just for kicks, he tried the spell again but nothing happened. The problem, of course, was that he didn't know if there was nothing to find or if he hadn't done the spell correctly.

With a shrug, he began to climb again.

What would he say to everyone when he got back? When he found all the keys, he assumed there would be a door—and that door would wake him up. He hoped so, anyway. Perhaps the quest for each key would teach him something new. He would wake and—would he be able to tell anyone on his YouTube channel what he'd been up to?

He had to, after all. A thing like this would be wildly popular. People would clamor to have their loved ones transferred to pods like this. His followers would definitely want to hear about it.

Those who still cared by then, of course. He hadn't put content out for weeks now so it was possible no one remembered him at all. His ad revenue would be shot to hell and he'd be behind on all the expansions.

And it wasn't like he even had friends to miss him. College

had been a mess of people he didn't like and didn't fit in with. There had only been one or two people he liked reasonably well, and they hadn't kept in contact since everyone graduated. Without having anything close to the means to rent an apartment in the Bay Area, Justin had stayed at home, so he hadn't had roommates or work friends, only the few friends who came back for holidays, and that was it.

"Justin." Zaara stood in front of him, her hands on her hips. She looked at him with a disapproving expression. "You're doing it again. Be honest, are you sick? Did the witch do something to you?"

"No. No, I'm only thinking. Oh…you were joking." His brain caught up with him and his cheeks flushed. "Sorry. I'm a little out of it today."

"Yeah, I can see that. Come on, we've hung the rabbit pelts out to dry and we'll get them on the way back. Speaking of which…" She walked him to a vantage point. "Lyle's seen motion in the ruins. We should be fairly well hidden here, but there's smoke drifting up, birds circling, and everything to suggest people are there."

"So?" he asked. When he realized what she meant, his stomach dropped. "Oh, I don't want to do this. I say we go, try to find the third key, and come back another time. Plus, we might learn more about who to trust that way."

"Justin, if there's a way to get a key, we should do it." She folded her arms. "Plus, she's right. Even the one we killed said they were bandits."

"They were trying to make a living. Ugh, this is *Les Misérables* all over again. I hated that book. No, don't ask. This one's not nearly as good as Luke Skywalker's story."

"I did like that one," Zaara said wistfully. "My point is, these bandits are people who would be out on the roads, robbing and murdering otherwise. Now they're wolves and they're attacking people's herds so the farmers can't make it through the winter.

Also, they are destroying the forest and the swamp, and the witch has the key."

"I agree," Lyle said.

"You said not to trust her," Justin pointed out.

"I'm not saying we should trust her. I'm saying we should kill the bandits."

Justin massaged his temples. His head was beginning to hurt.

"Or," a new voice said, "you could all come along quietly and no one will get hurt."

His head came up and his heart sank. Three bandits stepped out of the forest. No—he looked to one side and identified three more.

Two to one. He wasn't sure he liked those odds. On the other hand, whoever they were, they weren't friendly. He hopped from the wall and noted how quickly each bandit followed him with their gazes. The one on the far right was the slowest and he marked that.

"Why should we come with you?" he asked.

"I told you," the one who'd spoken before said. "So no one gets hurt."

"Ah," said Justin and promptly charged. "Stoooooooout!"

"That's my line!" Lyle yelled as he joined the battle.

"Stoooooooout!" Zaara yelled. A crackling noise and a yelp suggested she'd thrown a fireball.

"Both of you, stop it!" Lyle yelled. "My granda' will be spinning in his tomb!"

Justin slashed down with his sword and grimaced when the bandit he had targeted danced easily out of the way of his blade. Another ran face-first into his side, and although that seemed to hurt the attacker more than him, the heavy armor made it more difficult to recover from the impact.

He took the sword in both hands and whirled it wildly. The first bandit hadn't suffered so much as a scratch, but he stayed out of range and that was something. Others began to venture closer and he shifted the sword between hands to whip it out quickly to drive them back.

This wasn't a great stand-off for them, he had to admit. Triumphing in an outnumbered situation required the element of surprise, and they were already way past that point.

Also, the bandits seemed to have focused entirely on him, which was strange given that he could still hear his friends fighting. His head snapped around to look and, with a sinking sensation, he realized that there were no longer only six bandits.

Now, there were twelve.

"I think you can see that it would be best if you came with us," the leader said. He smiled and displayed teeth that seemed sharper than they ought to be.

"Not a chance," Zaara said tightly.

That was all Justin needed to hear. He wasn't of this world. For all he knew, it was better to go with them. If she didn't think so, however, he would go with her judgment. After all, she had kept herself safe on the road, alone and in an unfriendly town run by a crazy wizard.

He lunged and caught one of his adversaries in the leg. A fireball rocketed from his other hand and caught a second fully in the chest. The man dropped into the swamp with a scream and tried to put the flames out.

"That was a bad choice," the bandit leader snarled.

"Like we want to be taken as slaves?" Lyle retorted. Justin couldn't see his teammates from where he was, but a thud sounded a great deal like one of the dwarf's punches landing and was followed by a grunt of pain that he hoped came from a bandit.

Any chances of a peaceful resolution were gone, which made things a great deal simpler. He hacked, slashed, and fireballed his way through three more bandits. Zaara—or one of the female bandits—uttered a cry of pain before another fireball whooshed behind him.

Lyle, meanwhile, had decided that the best accompaniment to a good punching was to throw in a monologue about the parentage and proclivities of the bandit troupe, down to what they brushed their teeth with. Justin considered his particular suggestions on that last front to be improbable.

"Justin! Watch out!"

He threw himself sideways and barely avoided a battle-ax that descended with earth-shuddering force. His heart froze as he stared at it. How on earth would his brain react to thinking he'd been split in two by a battle-ax?

"Enough!" the bandit leader bellowed and to Justin's immense surprise, the next slash of his knives went to the wielder of the battle-ax. He collapsed in the mud with a gurgle and the leader pointed his bloody knives at everyone else. "All of you, enough. I said I wanted them taken alive and you three can stop trying to fight an impossible battle. Come on."

Justin was hauled unceremoniously out of the muck, his sword wrenched away, and his hands chained, and Lyle and Zaara joined him a moment later as captives.

"March," the leader said grimly, and the three of them stumbled forward, surrounded by a group of battered and manifestly unfriendly bandits.

CHAPTER ELEVEN

The experience of getting to New York was disturbingly smooth. The pilot at the private terminal knew Tad's face and they were airborne within five minutes of his arrival. A car was waiting when the plane taxied to a stop and he was whisked through the ever-present New York traffic with astonishing speed.

A young woman waited for him in the lobby of Diatek Industries. Her hair was cut in a severe bob, her dress revealed a strenuously thin form, and her genuine smile was disconcerting.

"Senator," she said.

"Did we speak on the phone?" he asked her and extended his hand.

"We did." She shook it warmly. "Please, this way."

In her presence, the security gate was opened without fuss and the two of them took an express elevator to what he could only think was the top level of the building. Wherever it was, it was high enough that his ears popped on the way.

The young woman led the way down a richly carpeted hallway to a set of frosted glass doors. Immediately, both tried to hold the doors open for one another. She laughed—again, shockingly warm in contrast to her appearance—and ushered him through and into a conference room. She did not enter and simply said, "The senator is here to see you, ma'am."

"Thank you, Lauren." The woman at the window turned to give her a smile before her gaze fixed on Tad. "Senator Williams. I'm glad you came. I'm Anna Price." She came to shake his hand.

She could have been an older version of her secretary. Also strenuously slim, she wore the kind of understated suit he had come to realize meant serious money. Her hair had once been blonde but was now more than half gray, although her eyes were a clear blue and her grasp was strong.

Tad settled into a chair when she gestured to the table and cleared his throat. He had decided on the plane to let her speak first. Caution meant he didn't want to give her any ideas or anything to seize on, especially since what Sylvia had managed to dig up was incredibly sparse.

Anna Price had studied chemistry at Harvard and went on to work for a pharmaceutical company for several years before she married. Her husband and daughter had both passed away, however, the daughter apparently from a car accident, and the husband some years later, potentially from heart problems. During the years between the two deaths, Anna had founded Diatek.

If there was little on Price, there was far more on Diatek—and none of it was particularly reassuring. The company had extensive contracts with the Department of Defense and the FBI. It had flown under the radar in terms of exerting influence regarding different legislation, but Tad could only think this was because the company had direct access to the officials making the decisions.

Price sat at the table and regarded him evenly. "It will save time, I think, if I tell you what I know about your situation. I know that your son, Justin, was involved in a car crash approximately six weeks ago and that he is now under the care of Dr.

Jean-Luc DuBois and the three operating members of a company called PIVOT. I can only assume he is still comatose and being treated using virtual reality.

"I know that, as of this morning, the FDA has arrested Jacob Zachary and given him twenty-four hours to shut the experiment down. I also know the leak of information to the FDA came from Dru Metcalfe, a lobbyist who works for several pharmaceutical companies, including the one that previously blacklisted Dr. DuBois's research. I know that Mr. Metcalfe has also leaked isolated details of Justin's treatment to the press. Would you say that is an accurate summation of your current situation?"

Tad clenched his teeth and gave a brief nod. This woman was businesslike and far too calm to be discussing matters of blackmail. It was almost like none of it shocked her.

He shouldn't have bothered to come.

Which was why he was surprised to hear Anna Price say, "What I believe you don't know, Senator, is that my daughter died under very similar circumstances. Like Justin, she was in a car accident. Like him, she was in stable condition. She was a fighter, Senator. Her name was Mina."

Startled, he looked at her. Her face was still and he could only now see the strain around her eyes.

"My husband and I were postgraduate students," Anna explained. "We didn't have much money and we tried everything we could. Both of us looked for different jobs. We sold our house, we sold everything we owned, and we lived out of our cars. We even tried to find research that might help Mina recover more quickly." She raised her chin fractionally. "We ran out of money. We went bankrupt, our postgraduate placements ended, and our next insurance companies would not take Mina. She died—not from her injuries but because we ran out of money to keep trying to save her."

His mouth hung open. In all analyses of what he might face, he had not expected this.

"The year after she died," Anna Price said, "I secured funding to open Diatek. My goal was very simple. I wanted to ensure that no other family would have to go through what ours had. I had worked for a pharmaceutical company and I knew the technologies that were being developed, but it wasn't an area of research that most companies were looking into, especially on the pharmaceutical side. It was always my focus. Diatek has made immense profits in other areas but all of them have been funneled into this research."

Tad swallowed. "I…see."

"Senator, I would like to fold PIVOT into Diatek Industries," Price said bluntly. "Their research and Justin's treatment would be covered indefinitely. I believe they are using an injection formula substantially similar to one we have clearance to test on human subjects. This would allow Justin's treatment to continue without interruption."

The silence dragged on as he looked at her for a long moment.

"You're wary," she said. It was not a question. "Given everything, I certainly can't blame you for that. Is there any particular area of concern I can address?"

He shrugged helplessly. "You know everything, which means you know why Dru Metcalfe is smearing me to the press."

"Yes." She raised her eyebrows.

"So you know my stance on blank checks and favors," he told her. "If you'll forgive me, your company came out of nowhere and were awarded a significant number of government contracts awfully quickly."

"Yes, that's true." She smiled bitterly. "You and I measure our morals differently, Senator. That is something you will need to come to terms with. I have made sacrifices in the name of progress and have collaborated on projects you would likely not find…ethical. I made my choice. I would not wish what happened to me—to my husband—on any other family."

"Your husband," Tad said and suddenly felt lost.

"He killed himself," Anna said crisply. He could see the precision masked an anguish that had not diminished even slightly with the years. "If I didn't have this, I might have done the same. I…was tempted."

He caught his breath and imagined the future stretching ahead. Years without Justin, where he knew that his son had not died because there was no treatment but because there was no money. The anger he already felt multiplied a hundred times and then a thousand times.

Anna's words struck a piece of him that was so raw, he wanted to press a hand over his chest.

And Mary…how would Mary take it?

Still, his reservations refused to be silenced.

"What's the catch?" Tad asked. Everything in him wanted to believe this was true, but Metcalfe had also offered the exact thing he wanted. This was even better, which he was sure meant the catch was even worse.

"There is no catch." Anna smiled now. It did not reach her eyes but given what they had discussed, he would have distrusted that even more. "I want to help, Senator. As I said, I have given a great deal to make sure other families do not face this same trial. The work done by Dr. DuBois and PIVOT is exceptional."

He considered this and nodded. "I…see." Half of him screamed to run and the other half yelled to take the deal. "Let me think about it, please."

"Of course." She did not seem surprised. Then again, he did not think she was surprised by very much. "You know how to reach me."

CHAPTER TWELVE

Justin woke in the freezing cold and his hands ached where he had curled them against his body. He couldn't determine why it was so bright or why there was so much wind. Cautiously, he opened his eyes for a moment, closed them against the glare, and opened them again as he sat far too quickly.

Dungeon cells were generally underground and deeply depressing, with a side helping of no-one-will-hear-you-if-you-scream. He had not enjoyed his brief stay in Riverbend's jail, and he hadn't looked forward to being in this one.

As things turned out, there was more than one way to keep someone in captivity. He wasn't chained, for instance, and his cell —such as it was—didn't have four walls. Whatever had happened to these ruins, the side of this building had sheared off and left it open to the wind.

Which, judging by the way it whistled and how close the fog lay, meant he was fairly high up. He estimated that it was at least ten stories, possibly more.

He struggled to remember the night before. The three of them had been brought to the ruins, at which point their weapons and armor had been taken and they'd been blindfolded. He didn't remember much after that beyond awkward stumbling over rocky ground and the sounds of muttered arguments about them. At some point, they'd been given food and water.

Of course, he hadn't noticed the bitter taste in the water until it was too late.

It was reassuring to find out he hadn't been killed, he decided morosely.

Now, if he could only find out what these bandits wanted, that would be a significant step in the right direction. He looked around. The floor wasn't particularly new but it didn't creak ominously when he moved across it either. He flattened himself onto his stomach and inched forward with what was probably excessive caution.

Still, despite the discomfort, excessive caution was better than being turned into jelly at the side of a tower.

And he definitely would be if he fell. Now that he was at the edge, he could see exactly how far up he was, and it was excessively high. He spared a thought for whoever had bothered to haul their unconscious bodies up a mountainside and so many flights of stairs before he recalled that this was a video game and they had probably simply been ported up.

Lucky bandits, he thought belligerently.

It occurred to him to wonder where the others were and if they'd been drugged.

"Zaara? Lyle?" He edged back to the wall. The floor might be stable, but he still preferred it there. "Anyone? Zaara?"

"Justin?" Her voice floated from his left. "Did you just wake up, too? Where are we?"

"Uh…are you afraid of heights?"

"Not really," she said promptly.

"Good. Because we're way the hell up in a tower." He pressed his back as far as it would go against the wall. What was the expression he'd once heard? *A fear of heights is illogical. A fear of falling from heights, on the other hand, is prudent.*

"That explains why they haven't bothered to keep us some-where with walls." She sighed. "Not to mention that I woke up when I almost fell through the floor."

His shoulders hunched around his ears. "Oh, God." Like he wasn't already feeling the sensation of falling, he now had to worry about the next time he fell asleep. What if he rolled? What if part of the floor collapsed and he couldn't wake up in time to grab onto something?

"I'd only have fallen one floor," Zaara told him, "but still." She sounded more grumpy than anything. "Where's Lyle?"

"I don't know, I can't hear him. Maybe he's on your other side."

"One moment. Lyle? Lyle?" A creaking sound suggested she was walking. "Lyle!" More creaking followed. "He's not over here —or he hasn't woken up yet. Given how well he can sleep ale off, though, I'd say he probably woke up before we did."

"Fair point." Justin considered this but not for long. "Okay, we need to find out where he is and if he's okay, but I don't think that's priority one. What we need to do first is find out why we're here. Or…maybe escape."

"I vote escape," Zaara said. "If they only wanted to do some friendly bargaining, there wouldn't have been any need for battle-axes. That was a good dodge, by the way. I don't think even your armor would have stopped that."

He shuddered. "I think you're right. Hmmm. You said there's a hole in the floor?"

"Yeah, why?"

"Well, maybe the door in the chamber below you isn't locked," he pointed out.

"Oh. Good point. Give me a moment." Scuffling sounds followed and he imagined her hanging upside down out of a hole in the ceiling. "I think you're right," she said, her voice muffled. "Okay, so I drop down, get out, and come get you."

"No, there might be patrols. Let's have you drop down and

then help me down as well." Although the thought of jumping so close to the edge was terrifying, the floor of the chamber below did extend somewhat farther.

"If you say so." She sounded dubious. "Okay, one sec—"

"Shhh!" he hissed suddenly. He could hear voices in the corridor outside and the dull thud of footsteps. A few seconds later, a key scraped in the lock and his door creaked open to admit the bandit leader. He stepped in and the door was closed and locked behind him.

"You're awfully confident," he observed and studied his captor. "I could tackle you off the edge."

His visitor only raised his eyebrows. Justin thought he saw something glimmering but the flicker of it was gone in the next moment.

"Why did you come to the ruins?" he asked.

"There was a job posting in East Newbrook," he said wearily. "Not even a job posting, really, merely someone saying there might be good loot in the ruins."

"Oh? And who was this someone?"

"I don't know. It was one of the pieces of paper the town crier put up." He threw his hands up. "Does it matter?"

"Given that this only turned into ruins two months ago and no one offered a reward? Yeah, it does." The bandit crouched to look him in the eyes.

"Wait, two months ago all of this was…fine?" He couldn't keep the incredulity out of his voice.

"Good acting," the bandit said derisively. He stood and wandered a few feet away. "Try again," he called over his shoulder. "And make it more believable this time."

He was distracted from his anger by the glimmer he saw again at the man's waist. Curious, he tried to picture a box lid opening as the witch had suggested, but nothing happened. Then, in a strange wash of inspiration, he remembered a summer day at the beach when a wave ebbed to show the stones and shells in its wake. As the water receded, the shoreline was revealed.

A chain of magic at the bandit's waist became instantly visible. Tendrils of magic extended up and down from it to burrow into his leather armor, and a trail led to the door. That was why he wasn't afraid, he realized—he knew that no matter what happened, he wouldn't go over the edge.

The man looked at his waist in surprise, then at his prisoner, and his eyes narrowed. "I knew it," he said. "The witch sent you."

"Oh?" Justin challenged. "Since you seem to be deciding everything about us, what then?"

"Then we kill you," he said bluntly.

A strained silence followed.

"If, on the other hand, you came on your own..." The man smiled and showed his teeth. "Maybe we can make a deal."

He considered his options. As far as he could tell, the best option was to play along for now, whether or not he intended to make a deal. That said, of course, was it better to admit their association with the witch or not?

His knowledge of magic was likely suspicious, he decided. He had to spill the beans.

"We set out from East Newbrook on our own," Justin said. "We planned to search the ruins for ancient artifacts. Yesterday, while trying to retrieve a donkey that had run away, we encountered a massive wolf. It and I fought and I wounded it, but it turned into a man, who told me a witch had cursed a group of bandits and that I could free them by killing her."

The bandit watched him suspiciously, his arms folded.

"We weren't sure what to do," he continued. "Shortly before we met you, we went off the road to a little shack, thinking there might be supplies we could use. It didn't look as if it had been inhabited in some time but a witch was inside. She held us captive with a spell and told us to find you and kill you—that you were killing the forest and, even before you preyed on flocks, you'd been bandits."

"She told you we were killing the forest?" Fury hardened his captor's tone. "No—that's her magic—her curse because she uses magic that isn't natural. She's the reason we became bandits. It wasn't our choice. She wanted our town and our tower, so she fought us for it. That's the reason for the ruins, and she cursed us when she couldn't drive us out. We're bandits now because it's not safe to be around humans. When the change comes over us… we can't always control ourselves. Sometimes, we attack."

Justin stared at him, genuinely torn now.

"She needs to die," the man said fiercely. "This tower was ours for the taking and it's not like she had any more right—" He broke off. "We have a potion," he stated coldly. "It will incapacitate her and make her weak enough to kill. None of us can use it as her curse alerts her to our presence. But you could do it. You could free us all. We'll give you a day to decide."

The door opened to let him through and slammed again behind him before the loud footsteps of the bandit group walked away. He peered out the tiny opening in the door but didn't see any shadows to suggest a guard had remained.

"Zaara, did you hear that?"

"Every word. How did he know you were sent by the witch?"

"I used the spell she taught us," he explained. "I finally made it work." He slumped against the wall. "I have no idea who to trust, though. Did you hear what he said? About how she had no more right to this place than they did?"

"Yes." Her voice was contemplative. "I did, now that you mention it."

"What do you think?" Justin asked her.

"I'm…not sure. If we have to side with one, I guess I'd side with her. If she were someone like Sephith, she'd have lackeys to help her fight the wolves, wouldn't she? Or she'd simply be able to kill them. And whatever they were doing before, they're hurting more people now."

"Wait." He peered at the wall. "What you just said—if we have to side with one. What if we didn't?"

"Wait, what?"

"What we need is information, right?" he asked her. "We need to get out of here, take the potion, and find out who's right before we deal with anyone." He listened and waited, but she made no response. "What do you think?"

"Let's do it," Zaara agreed.

CHAPTER THIRTEEN

Mary looked at the clock for what felt like the twelfth time in twenty minutes.

She sighed when she realized it had only been ten minutes.

The building's owners had been able to restrict the FDA agents from entering again by citing the exact language of what appeared to be an injunction, although she didn't fully understand it. From the snippets of discussions she'd picked up, it seemed the entire process reeked of corruption and power plays. Whether this was true or not was moot on some level. Yes, they could fight it, but whoever had orchestrated it had done so with a time limitation in mind. When the twenty-four hours were up, they would have no legal grounds to keep them out.

Jacob, back from jail on bond, was cloistered with Nick and Amber as they conference-called with the lawyer. Mary had tried to sit in on some of the meetings, but between the technical terms being thrown around and her guilt, she wasn't much of a help at this point.

It didn't improve her mood that she wasn't useful at all. She couldn't help the PIVOT team, she couldn't help DuBois prep

Justin for a potential move, and she couldn't help Tad with his work in the senate.

She looked at the clock for the thirteenth time. Only twelve hours and forty-two minutes were left.

A light touch on her shoulder startled her and she turned, expecting to see Tad there—hopefully with perfect news.

It was DuBois, though. She hoped her face didn't fall too obviously and cleared her throat. "Can I help with anything?" she asked him.

"No. But I can help you. I can put you back in the game."

Mary stared at him. "Are you…sure? Can you do that?"

"No," Amber called from the side of the room. "He can't. But we're all screwed anyway so I say go for it."

"Ms. Garcia, please don't say things like that while I'm on the line." The lawyer sounded pained.

"Oh. Right. Sorry. Mary, don't go into the game. Help the doctor clean up. DuBois, stop suggesting things you know are illegal." She gestured at the older woman, then the pod, and gave the man a thumbs up.

Mary smiled, but her eyes stung with unshed tears. These three kids weren't much older than Justin, and they were utterly prosaic about their chances of facing legal action. She let DuBois usher her to the pod and sat.

Tina flashed into her mind. For now, the girl was a blank, a faceless entity. She hadn't looked up her social media profiles and preferred to avoid the chance that she would send an angry message. To control the rising snarl of fury, she pressed her fists hard into the soft bottom of the pod and tried to push the thoughts aside. These people put their livelihood on the line for Justin, and where was Tina? Off Scott-free and uninjured although she claimed she was miserable.

The girl wasn't miserable enough, she decided.

"Mrs. Williams?" DuBois looked concerned. He held sterilizing wipes in his gloved hands as he frowned at her. "Are you all right?"

She thought of snapping a response that it was a ridiculous question, but she held her tongue. The doctor had his moments but he meant no harm—and he did the best he could to help her now. He had noticed her worry and it would concern him as he was putting her into the game. That was what she had to focus on. He was doing all he could to give her the time with Justin she desperately wanted.

"I'm…yes, I'm all right." She forced a smile.

He nodded, but he left an expectant silence as he swabbed her temples and wrists.

"I'm thinking about the woman who was with Justin in the car," she explained.

"Was she killed?" he guessed.

"No," Mary said bitterly. "No, she's fine."

"That's a relief." DuBois smiled at her. "Did you know her well?"

"I barely knew her and it's not—" *It is not a relief.* Mary cleared her throat. She held one wrist out for an adhesive pad. "Her parents and I set her up with Justin. She was driving the night of the accident, was going way too fast, and crashed the car. The girl is fine and Justin is like this." She gestured at the pod with her free hand.

To her surprise, DuBois still did not speak. He looked briefly at her as he put the pad on her other wrist and then began to position the neural pads around the sides of her face and at the base of her skull.

"I don't want to wish pain on her," she continued. "But it isn't fair. She reaches out to me constantly for news about Justin and I can't bear to write back. I can't—she has no idea of the pain she's put us all through. Tad and I are in hell, you and the rest of the team might wind up in jail, and none of it would have happened if she'd been careful."

The doctor nodded now. Instead of hooking her up to the machine, he took a seat nearby. "I know that feeling," he said.

"You do?" she asked, surprised.

He nodded again, his expression thoughtful. "It felt unfair when my research was shut down the first time." He held a hand up and took a very long time to choose his words. When he spoke, his voice was oddly flat and she could see how hard it was for him to try to understand the twists and turns inside someone else's mind.

"I understand that it's not the same as having a child in a coma. But I think it may be more similar than you think. I don't mean to be disrespectful, not at all. That project was my life's work. I enjoyed it because it was difficult, but I also toured hospitals and saw people in comas and their families. I did everything right so I could help them because I believed that what I needed to do was create the treatment." He shook his head and she saw that the fallout still did not make sense to him on a fundamental level. "I spent every day for years working on that research. I handpicked my team and I never took a day off. When it was shut down, it wasn't that I had done anything wrong. It was something totally meaningless, and it would cost so many people their lives."

Mary hunched her shoulders. DuBois seemed so vague that she had never considered that he might feel this way.

"You seemed so calm about it," she said hesitantly.

"It's been years since then." He smiled at her and then, as if to assure her that he was still the same person she'd known all this time, he stripped his gloves off and pulled out a bag of popcorn. "And most of this stuff...well, it took me a year before I could even go into the lab," he added as he munched on a handful of caramel corn. His low-key demeanor did not match the words but she could see that he meant it.

"What changed?"

"I realized that continuing to be angry would accomplish

nothing," he said. "Other researchers didn't understand. They told me projects were called off for all kinds of reasons and I shouldn't be angry. That wasn't a good reason to me. Why would I feel less bad to know that other lifesaving projects had been shut down for bad reasons? It only made me feel worse." He looked completely baffled. "What did make me feel better was realizing that nothing I could do would change the fate of that project. I only had the skills to do research, and if I stayed in my apartment and was angry all day, I wouldn't do any research."

Mary considered this.

"I didn't like being that angry," DuBois explained. "I blamed myself for things that did not make sense at all. I would tell myself that if I had studied law, maybe I would know how to appeal things better than my university—even though if I had been a lawyer, the project would never have existed at all. I thought about what would have happened if I'd gone to one of those companies. Maybe if the treatment was beneficial to them, they wouldn't have stopped it. But I couldn't go back in time."

"You can't change the past," she agreed. How many times had she read that sentiment in celebrity interviews and self-help books?

"Exactly," he said as if she had come up with the quote on her own. "That is a good way to put it. I could not change the past and it was no use being angry at myself for not knowing different areas of study."

"I have felt useless," she admitted. "I don't understand the technology, I'm not a doctor, and I can't help Tad with any of this. I don't know what to do except feel guilty that all of you are in this mess…" She hung her head. "I've failed my child, Doctor. I can't help him."

"You can't?" DuBois fixed her with a firm look. "I don't think that's correct, Mrs. Williams. You and your husband chose together to find the best doctors you could and placed Justin in our care. You made sure the team was functioning well. You brought food in and I remember you telling Jacob to sleep. You told us things we could put in the game to make him happy." He shook his head. "I am not sure why you think you cannot help him. You have been helping him. All of us, too."

Mary shook her head. "I...don't know if I'll ever really be able to believe that," she admitted. The rest came out in a rush, an admission she hadn't even shared with Tad. "I don't go to confession anymore. I'm afraid the priest will hear how angry I am. I'm afraid God will hear how angry I am. I would never want someone else's parents to suffer for this, but I wish it was Tina in a coma and not Justin. It isn't fair and it doesn't make sense."

"I imagine she feels the same way," DuBois said neutrally.

She studied him silently for a moment. "She...does," she admitted. "She told me so in an email."

"Can you imagine writing that email?" he asked. His face was distant and contemplative. It wasn't a rhetorical question and he was not making a point. He was imagining it. "She emails you to ask how he is. She wants him to be better because she does not think it is fair that he was injured and she was not. She is...miserable." He nodded as if checking an equation and realizing that it balanced. "She also knows that you are in pain and wishes she could take it away."

Mary said nothing. She felt the first stirrings of guilt.

"You could tell her that he is improving," he suggested. "We have seen measurable improvement. Maybe it would help her to know that."

Her lips twitched in a strange smile. DuBois was very good at putting the pieces together but he still didn't understand—not really. He could not comprehend the outward force of her anger or her desire to have Tina be miserable.

And, with his simple, easy suggestion, she felt her anger unwind somewhat. She remembered the moment when she'd stood in her kitchen and realized that to wish the coma on Tina was to wish her anguish on her parents. She didn't want that.

And when she thought of the girl, she saw now that she'd wished grief on her without ever really thinking about that grief.

She remembered being young. How would she feel if it were Tad in a coma and she was at fault? She couldn't imagine that and she swallowed uncomfortably.

"Thank you," she told DuBois. She took his hand and squeezed it. "Thank you."

"Of course." He stood and motioned for her to lie back.

"Please…will you pull me out if Tad calls?" she asked.

The doctor nodded and she had the sense that he would take her directive seriously. He wouldn't let her linger in the game if it were bad news.

His assurance was comforting.

Mary closed her eyes and breathed out. Her vision began to fuzz into pure white, and in seconds, the feed from the video game took over. She did not see DuBois shut the lid of the pod but she was smiling.

Soon, she would see Justin again.

CHAPTER FOURTEEN

"I want to say," Zaara called over the wall, "that if I die by falling through the floor, I'll be really angry about it."

"Only briefly, though," Justin responded. "Look on the bright side."

"Very funny." She grunted, followed by the crack of wood. "Ow. And no, I didn't fall."

"That's good to know." He sat cross-legged and drummed his fingers nervously on the floor. "Let me know when you're down."

"Uh-huh."

"Are you waiting for something?"

"I'm having an argument with my better sense," she muttered in a rough and strained tone. From the sound of it, she was halfway through the hole and held herself up on her elbows. "This is beginning to seem like a very bad idea."

"Leaving on our own seems like a much better idea than letting them send us out," Justin told her. "They'll keep something we care about to make sure we come back, and I'm kind of worried that something will be you or Lyle."

"So the 'we' is you?"

"In this case, yes. They did come to speak to me."

"For all you know…" Zaara panted and he waited. "They talked to Lyle too. Good gods, I wonder if he sold us out. I'll stab him if he did. All right, here goes nothing." The sound of ripping cloth preceded an oath, a thud, and another muttered expletive.

"Zaara? Zaara!"

"Ow." He heard limping footsteps. "Ow, ow, ow. They couldn't put pillows down, could they? Nooooooo…"

Justin's mouth twitched. He decided to focus on that as he inched toward the edge of the floor. While he'd asked Zaara what she was waiting for, the truth was that he was none too eager to do his part. He thought of asking her to sneak up the stairs and let him out, pictured what she would say in response to that, and decided to take his chances with the several-hundred-foot drop instead.

Cautiously, he stuck his head over the edge. "Are you ready?"

The area below their cells was one large chamber and she stood under where he lay. She took a careful step to the side and gave him a thumbs-up. One sleeve was ripped down the side and a nasty bruise was already visible but otherwise, she seemed fine.

"Okay," he said. "Right. Okay. Right. Okay." He maneuvered his legs to the edge. "Right." He lay on his stomach and stared at the grain of the wood. "Okay."

"Justin?"

"Yep. I'm, uh…having an existential crisis."

"I don't know what that is." Zaara sounded exasperated. "Are you worried about falling off the tower?"

"Yes."

"Well, get over it." She didn't sound particularly sympathetic. "Now-ish would be good."

"Maybe this plan was a mistake."

"Right, I'll jump through the hole in the floor again, then." She came to peer toward the edge of the ledge. He couldn't see her, of course, but he could feel the force of her stare. "Are you kidding me, you good-for-nothing, pot-lid-wearing—I don't even know…useless, fireball-slinging donkey-wrangler?"

Justin sighed. He was fairly sure he could hear the AI laughing and that annoyed him. "Right. I'm coming down. Grab my hand, right?"

"Oh, you mean the goal is to stop you from going over the edge? Huh. I hadn't understood that." Her tone was as sweet as poison. "So help me, you will jump or I will come up there and make you wish you had."

"Right. Okay. Right. Okay."

"Stop saying that!"

"Okay." He wiggled his legs off the edge of the floor, listened to the wind whistling, and tried not to whimper pathetically. Stupidly, he told himself he should be glad she wasn't real because if she were, he'd have sunk any chances he had with her. He wiggled back farther, inch by careful inch. With his arms braced on the wood and his fingers scrabbling for purchase, he let his body hang before he grasped the edge of the floor and exhaled as he let himself down. His feet dangled a meter or so above the floor.

When Zaara began to back away, he knew the panic showed on his face because she sighed.

"Listen, you dolt, I'll grab your hand and pull you this way. Got it?"

"Oh. That's a good plan. Right."

"If you say 'okay' one more time—"

Justin pressed his lips together, prayed deeply, and released the wood. He struck the floor, threw himself forward, and sighed when he realized he wasn't still moving. Zaara had hold of both of his hands but the floor had held.

Or so he thought. With a crack and a shudder, the boards under him splintered and he felt the sickening sensation of freefall.

"Whoa—whoa!" She threw herself back, her boots braced on

the floor. "Justin, throw your leg up over the edge. *Now!* I'm sliding. Justin!"

His hands slipped in hers but he managed to hook one foot onto a stable piece of a beam and wrenched both himself and Zaara sideways. She grimaced with the effort of hauling him up and tried to brace her boots on the weather-beaten wood flooring. The beam gave them enough space for them to gain better purchase and for him to scramble to safety. With one hand still clasped around his forearm, she wrenched the door open and the two of them tumbled into the hallway as the rest of the floor crumbled behind them.

A long pause followed.

"Do I want to look behind me?" his companion asked. She was close to hyperventilating.

"I don't think so." Justin looked cautiously over his shoulder and saw wind whistling and far too steep a drop. Bile rose reflexively. "Oh, God. You definitely don't want to look. I regret that."

"Okay, this way." She crawled toward the stairs. "Shut the door."

He shut it behind him, latched it, and pushed to his feet. His hands and legs were trembling and he began to laugh.

"Holy shit. Oh, God, that was such a bad idea."

Zaara laughed too. "Yeah, probably."

"Hello?" a voice called.

The teammates froze.

"Marco?"

Justin grimaced and only narrowly avoided saying, "Polo."

"Marco, is that you?"

He buried his face in his hands and tried not to laugh. The struggle continued when Zaara grabbed him by his shirt and began to drag him up the stairs.

"Now is not the time," she snapped in his ear.

Although he nodded, between the adrenaline and the name, he couldn't seem to stop. The two climbed the stairs as quickly as they could. He stumbled sometimes when he laughed too hard to lift his foot properly and she continually darted worried looks behind them.

Two floors up, she stopped to rest her ear against a door. She peered through the latch, nodded, and motioned him up the stairs.

"If you can't be useful, hide."

"I'll…I'll take care of him. By way of apology." Justin gestured for her to hide instead. He waited and bounced on the balls of his feet until the guard's footsteps drew closer. With the wind outside the tower and the creak of stone and wood, he wasn't surprised that the man wondered whether he'd heard something or not.

"Marco?" the guard called. "Marco, is that—" He stepped around the corner and stared at Justin, open-mouthed.

"Polo," he said cheerfully and punched him in the face. The man fell like a sack of bricks and he caught the front of his vest and dragged him onto the landing. When Zaara opened the door into a room that was fully enclosed, they took the opportunity to drag the unconscious body in before they began to strip him as fast as they could.

His armor, luckily, fit Justin well—or maybe that was merely the video game auto-sizing things. Given how tall the werewolves seemed to be, that was probably the case. It meant that he now had greaves, wrist guards, and a helmet, as well as a leather buckler and two knives for Zaara, although she gave him one for now.

They snuck out of the room, closed the door, and used a piece of loose wood to wedge the handle closed.

"We should go down," she mouthed and gestured to illustrate the point.

Justin gave a thumbs up and they descended. Given that he was now dressed as a guard, he went first. Two floors down from their cells, the corridor divided, straightened, and wound into utter blackness, punctuated only by flickering lanterns.

"It must be cut into the rock," Zaara said quietly. "What now?" She pointed at the stairs. "Down, or in?"

"If the tower's crumbling and they have treasure, it's probably in here," Justin said, after a moment. "Like that potion and…well, my sword, which I need if we fight werewolves. It's the only thing that hurt the last one, remember. So let's try this way."

They set off as quietly as they could. She moved purposefully, but her fingers constantly moved to where her knives should be and she looked surprisingly small without her breastplate and cloak. Funnily enough, however, with a white blouse and black leather pants, she could pass for someone in the real world. He hid his smile and didn't mention that to her.

They were halfway down the hall when they heard something that made both of them prick up their ears.

"Aaaaaand the miners heaved, and the miners hauled—"

Lyle might not have a future as a singer, but his voice was certainly distinctive. The friends exchanged a hopeful glance before they snuck closer to a door, which they found locked and heavily barred. It didn't look as if the dwarf was held in luxury.

A second later, both of them jumped when he said, "Whoever's sneaking around out there, I can hear ye."

Justin gestured to the door and motioned for Zaara to pick the lock. She folded her arms at him, sighed, and retrieved the set of keys the guard had carried.

"Oh, right. That is better."

"Yeah. Yeah, it is." She tried a few keys before one slid in and turned, then pushed the door open and motioned for him to go first.

The room inside was pitch-black. He came up short and looked around as she ran smack into him.

"Aren't ye a little short for a werewolf?" Lyle asked.

"Huh?" He stared in the direction of his voice. "Oh, the helmet." He took it off. "It's us. We're here to save you."

"Are ye now?" The prisoner hopped down from where he'd been seated—a boulder, judging by the shape. "About time. I was getting bored, you know."

"Yes, yes." Justin gestured dismissively. "Do you have any idea why they didn't have you out with us on the outside of the tower?"

"My guess? They assume I know enough about masonry to have escaped." Lyle looked around the hallway and pointed farther into the mountain. "There's gold thataway. Anyway, they put me in a room with no joins and no hinges. I have to say, it was well-done. I went over that thing three times and never found so much as a crack to work with."

Justin made a mental note to learn more about Dwarven magic and led the way down the hallway. In whispers, he and Zaara caught their teammate up on what was going on.

"I don't see why we don't kill all of 'em," Lyle said when they were done.

"Because we don't know who's to blame yet." He gave him a horrified glance.

"They've all got the look to 'em," he retorted. "Every one of 'em has dirtied their hands, let me tell you."

"So we simply kill them?"

"Why not?" Lyle sounded quite self-assured. He stopped at a door that blended into the rock. "This is the treasure." He ran his fingers around the edge, found the hidden catches, and pushed it open with a kick. As he took a torch from the wall, he said, "They'd kill you straight off. You know they wouldn't even hesitate."

"That's not the point!" he protested as he followed him into the room.

"If that's not the point what the hell is?" The dwarf gave him a confused look.

Justin had no idea how to respond to that, so he looked around the room instead.

His jaw dropped at what he saw. Not only was their armor and weaponry in a neat pile in the center of the room, but his friend had also been correct that there was gold. It wasn't Aladdin's cave levels of gold, but there were coffers that didn't close properly, more suits of armor lining one wall, and whole racks of weaponry.

The group scrambled to arm themselves. Zaara sighed with relief as she donned her armor once more and flashed him a sunny smile.

"It doesn't feel right not to have some protection."

He snickered internally and managed to not make a joke about that as he pulled his plate armor on. Lyle sifted through handfuls of jewelry and once in a while, flung a piece toward one of them with an explanation of why. One ring set with a ruby apparently increased one's ability to strike true, and a silver chain granted the wearer strength. Zaara got a bracelet that made her "light of foot," in Lyle's words, and she paused to stare at the young man's wrist.

"I wonder why they didn't take your amulet," she said and pointed to where the blue amulet was still on his wrist.

Justin looked down in a panic. He was also confused but he hadn't thought how difficult it would be if he were to lose this now when he couldn't exactly return to Riverbend easily and find another. "I don't know why they didn't take it off," he responded after a moment.

"Oh, they tried," the AI told him. "Four of them were full-on electrocuted. It was hilarious—I mean…sad."

He bit his lip to keep from laughing when something moved in the shadows and he stumbled back. His feet caught and in an effort to stay upright, he upended a suit of armor nearby and wasn't able to catch it in time. Everyone in the room covered their ears as it clanged.

"Justin?"

He knew that voice.

"Mom?" He scrambled to his feet. Again, it was jarring to see her not looking like his mother but he knew it was her. "What's going on? Why are you here?"

"I...came to see...you." She looked around. "Is something wrong?"

"Well, for one thing, I heard an alarm bell go off," Lyle said.

"Fuck," Justin said furiously.

"Justin! Language!"

"Mom?" He looked at her. "We're about to have a whole crowd of angry werewolves in here."

"Oh," Mary said. "Fuck."

CHAPTER FIFTEEN

"Mom!" Justin called. "Find something to fight with."

"Oh. Right." Mary looked around, then at the ceiling. "Oh, thank you," she said to no one.

"Was that the AI?" he asked wearily.

"Yes." She smiled. "It's very helpful. It told me I'll want something made of silver and also how to throw something called a death-coil."

"You have to be kidding me."

"Try being pleasant for once."

He glared upward to the imagined location of the AI. When this was over, he would find who had created it and they would have to answer some serious questions.

The clatter and clang of feet very quickly changed into the pound of paws and the howling of wolves.

"Fuck," Zaara said under her breath. She stood in the corner of the room.

"What are you doing?" he demanded.

"Looking for something silver," she told him. "I can't find anything."

"Take this." Mary threw a silver ring at her. "Unless you want this. Yes, you'd probably better have that." She tossed the dagger and Zaara lobbed the ring back.

He looked on, shook his head at the bizarreness of it, and looked at the door. "Are you ready to do this, Lyle?"

"Yeah. Are you? Last I heard, you didn't think people trying to kill you was a good enough reason to kill them."

"That is not what I said. You said they would kill me if they had the chance. When someone's actively trying, all bets are off."

"That doesn't make any—"

"Later, Lyle!"

The first wolf skidded through the doorway and Justin swung his sword overhand. An animal scream was quickly cut off as the beast was pushed out of the way by the momentum of the others behind it. Justin wrenched his sword free and slashed sideways.

Lyle charged into the fray, silver flashing at his knuckles, and pounded his fists into his first target. Yips mixed with battle cries and Zaara leapt into the battle from overhead.

"Justin!" Mary dragged him out of the way and launched a bolt of something black and deadly looking out of one palm. "Stay behind me."

"Are you crazy, woman? I'm the one in the plate armor."

"I'm invulnerable," she told him. "I hope."

"You hope—*Mom!*"

A wolf reared and lashed out with both claws, only to slide off her as a blue shield illuminated across her skin. The beast snarled and danced back and she threw another bolt of black magic at its face. "See?" she shouted at her son.

"I hope Dad's watching this," he muttered. He slid around her side and stabbed a wolf directly in the chest but retreated hastily when its jaws snapped dangerously close to his face. "Oooof, that was a slim margin. Fuck."

"Justin, you know how I feel about you swearing."

"Mom, you're throwing death bolts."

The last remaining wolf snarled, adjusted its shoulders, and screamed as Zaara rolled under its belly and sliced it with the silver knife. It collapsed and she waved a hand at the other three. "Come on!"

They sprinted out of the room and into the hallway.

"Will we make it?" Justin asked breathlessly as they ran. His muscles were on fire.

"I gotta be honest, I have no idea, and—oh, *shit*!" Zaara skidded to a halt when they heard the sound of boots on the stairs. "That is way too many—run! The other way."

"We don't know what's the other way," he protested.

"Is there a way out?" Mary asked.

"Mom, I don't—you're asking the AI, aren't you."

"She says it's this way." His mother caught his wrist and yanked him along.

"You know, I don't think I'll tell my YouTube subscribers about this part," he said contemplatively. Snarls and yips grew more frenzied behind them, mixed with the clangs that suggested the soldiers were bursting out of their armor as they transformed.

"Less talking and more running." Lyle chugged along at their side and reminded Justin of nothing so much as a pug. When he caught the glint in the dwarf's eye, he revised his opinion from pug to terrier.

The group pounded down the hallway and without warning, slid off the edge and down a flight of stairs into utter darkness.

"Ow!" That sounded like Zaara.

"I—oof, fuck. Are you okay?" Justin couldn't tell which way was up anymore. He constantly tried to catch hold of a handrail but didn't think there was one.

"Of course I'm not okay. You're heavy in that armor. Lyle?"

"Relax," the dwarf responded. "I've been through a ton of these. Relax, let go, and think of happy things."

"You are out of your mind." Justin gasped a breath. "Fuck, how long is this staircase?"

"The AI says not much longer," Mary replied. "Zaara, grab my hand, I think I can—"

"*Ow!*" With thuds and clanks, all four of them stopped abruptly. The wolves shuffled around at the top of the stairs but they couldn't be sure if the beasts wanted to try coming down.

"A door," Justin said wildly. "Get it open."

"There's no door!" Zaara told him sharply.

"Are you sure? Wait, why aren't you looking? Lyle!"

"There's no door," the dwarf echoed.

"You're telling me someone carved the world's longest staircase and it goes nowhere?" He made a fireball in one hand and glared at Lyle. "There is a door here. Find it."

"Do you see a door?" His friend gestured at the blank stone wall with surprising elegance.

"No, I...oh." He stared at the wall, closed his eyes, and breathed out as he pictured waves on the beach, but his effort was disturbed.

A yip and some scuffling told him the wolves had started down the stairs and his head jerked around.

"Focus," Zaara yelled.

"What about you?" Despite his challenge to her, he forced himself to refocus. *Waves in, waves out. Don't think about the horde of angry wolves.* This was hard. *In, out. Keep the fireball going. Wolves. In, out. In...out.*

"It's there!" Lyle caught him by his armor and yanked him through the door. "You go, you go, you go...all here, okay." He slammed the door shut with his shoulder and a moment later, they were treated to the immensely satisfying sound of several wolves careening into a stone wall at high speed.

"Ah. Perfection." He blew a breath out. "Everything hurts. Does everyone else hurt everywhere?"

"I do," Zaara said.

"Not really." Mary sounded remarkably calm. "I am a little dizzy, though. Wait…no, I'm not. Thank you, AI."

"Unbelievable," Justin muttered. "Okay, all, let's find a way out of here. I think we can safely say going the other way is off the table."

CHAPTER SIXTEEN

Justin's ball of flame guided them partway down the corridor, although his mother noticed it kept burning his hand. It wasn't far, however, before they found old, unused torches on the wall. Zaara retrieved one and lit it from the fireball before she strode away to find others. With everyone now armed with light, they set off again.

Mary looked around as they walked. The walls weren't marked and dust lay thickly on the floor. Whatever this place was, it hadn't been used in a very long time.

"What do you think this is?" Justin asked, his mind running along similar lines to hers. "The air…doesn't seem as stale as it should."

"Yer right, and that's good," Lyle said. "A closed-off mine is the worst place you can be." His voice showed the depth of his feeling. "It's part of why I left," he added gruffly after a moment.

He glanced at his friend but held his tongue, which Mary approved of. The dwarf's fear was obviously deep-seated and she had a sense that he wasn't someone who made admissions like this lightly. After all, he'd been remarkably unsentimental during the fight.

She shook her head. What was she thinking? Lyle wasn't real. He was a fake person created by the makers of the game—perhaps shaped by Justin's choices, but not real.

Unwillingly, her gaze drifted to Zaara.

While she hated to say it, she could see what her son saw in the girl. Her appearance wasn't the first thing you noticed about her. Rather, it was the way she walked—not the confidence she projected as she tried to be a dangerous outlaw but the real confidence that lay beneath. Behind the black armor and double daggers, she was watchful and protective, as well as brave. She'd been the one who ran down the corridor first, after all, even knowing they would likely face opposition.

Mary was lost in her thoughts when she heard the strange skittering sound from the darkness ahead.

Everyone froze and only the flames from the torches continued to dance and send their shadows flickering over the walls. She peered into the tunnel ahead of them and realized she was holding her breath. The battle with the wolves hadn't affected her as much as she'd expected, not with the realization that she was immune to damage.

This, though… Something about an enemy lurking and not knowing what it was made it more difficult.

She thought she saw a gleam in the pitch-black shadow and leaned forward. A pair of eyes appeared, then another pair. The two of them must be close together, and they were very far off the ground.

When she saw the other four eyes, she uttered a little sound of fear.

More than anything, she hated spiders and always had. She was a country girl and had gutted deer and fish, mucked stables out, and planted and harvested in every kind of weather imaginable. There was a time when she used to catch snakes and bring them inside.

But she couldn't stand spiders.

"What do you want to bet," Justin said slowly, "that it's poisonous?"

Mary resisted the urge to clap her hands over her face—which wouldn't be good, given the fact that she carried a torch.

"I'd say the odds are good," Lyle said.

Zaara nodded.

"So I'd propose we burn it," he said and looked at Zaara, then at Mary. "Zaara and I will throw fireballs. Do you want to join in with some of your death bolts, Mom?" He gave her a crooked smile she remembered from his childhood. "Maybe you'll feel braver around spiders if you help deal with—"

"Justin!" Zaara yelled.

The spider had come down the hallway in a rush as if sensing the team's distraction.

Mary screamed as loudly as she could and threw her hands out. The torch tumbled into the dust and black power poured out of her, flanked by bolts of flame from Zaara and Justin.

The three strikes were more than enough to kill the creature but not enough to halt its momentum. It uttered an unearthly shriek as it caught fire but still skittered forward at high speed. His mother gave another full-volume scream of her own before he tackled her sideways against the wall as the flaming body went past.

"Mom. Mom!"

She managed to stop screaming. "What?"

"You're deafening me," he told her but laughed as he held one hand up to shield his eyes and studied the spider. After a moment, he turned her away and marched her down the hall. "I wouldn't look if I were you. Suffice it to say it's taken care of. Come on, everyone. Zaara, if you'd take the front?"

"Right-o." The young woman grinned and handed Mary's torch to her before she added shyly, "And I don't suppose you could teach me that spell, could you? I've never even seen that one."

"Uh…"

"She'll think about it," Justin said firmly. He draped an arm around his mother's shoulders and steered her down the hallway behind the other two. "How about that, huh? You killed the spider to end all spiders. My mom, the spider-slayer. Did you get any levels from that?"

"Levels?" she asked. She still tried to calm the racing of her heart.

Blue letters popped up on one side of the screen, reading **FEAR SLAYER, Level 1**.

"Oh. I guess I'm a Fear Slayer."

"That's cool," he said encouragingly. "As you do more and more, you'll level up."

"As I do more?" She thought she might have a heart attack. "How do you survive this game? Good God above."

Justin laughed and hugged her. "Dad's not gonna believe this unless he's watching it right now." He looked at her and some of what she felt must have shown on her face because he said slowly, "Is everything okay? And why did you disappear like that last time?"

"Oh, I…" Mary cleared her throat and couldn't decide what to tell him. The thought of him being closed in darkness without this world around him and without friends was terrifying—and surely it would be more terrifying for him without knowing what was happening. But then again, if Tad and the others found a way to avert this, he might spend the rest of his time in this world waiting for an ax to fall, and surely that would be cruel.

She considered what to say, conscious that he was waiting.

Finally, she patted his hand. "We miss you," she said. "Putting many people in the game at once isn't something they had a good idea how to do, you see. They want to be sure everything is working. I was glad to test it, of course, but I don't want to be selfish and get in the way of your progress."

"You're not getting in the way," Justin said stoutly.

"Oh, really?" Mary raised an eyebrow. "Having your mother come along with you on your adventures isn't getting in the way?"

The light wasn't very good, but she was sure she saw him blush and Lyle cleared his throat in a way that might have been a stifled laugh.

"Mom," he said, embarrassed.

"You don't need me here," she said. As the words emerged, she realized she truly meant them—and that, in a way, she was glad. "You're doing well, Justin. I heard you speaking to—Lyle, is it? Yes—about when you should kill and when you should not. I like that you hesitate." She smiled at him. "Tell me about who we were fighting back there."

"I assume you mean the wolves," he said wryly. "I have no idea if the spider had a backstory."

"Oh, do you have to bring it up?" Mary groaned.

"Sorry, sorry." He grinned. "Ah, the wolves…long story short, there's a pack who were probably turned into werewolves by a witch. They want us to kill her so they can be set free of the curse. She wants us to kill them because she says they were robbing people and they're cursing the forest. We have no idea who's right."

She nodded. The corridor had begun to slope up slightly as they walked and it wound gently into a curve. So far, thankfully, nothing else moved in the darkness.

Justin was different here. She could hardly believe how much, in fact. No, not different. She considered the best definition.

More. She looked at briefly him, then looked away. Would he remember this when he recovered?

She hoped so and that he would be this person when he returned. He had always been smart and able to determine the best course of action. Now, though, he was decisive, willing to share his opinion and argue for it, or even take control of the situation when it was needed. Clearly, he wasn't using the video game as an excuse to go on a murdering spree and as far as she could tell, he hadn't even made a move on Zaara.

Though DuBois had been evasive when she asked about that.

With a sigh, she conceded that it was none of her business.

"Is something wrong?" Justin asked her. "Seriously, Mom."

"I have to say that when I saw you playing all those games, this isn't quite what I imagined."

He smiled. "Yeah. Me, neither." He lowered his voice slightly. "I told Zaara and Lyle the truth, kind of, but they mostly think I'm crazy. I mean…you know what I mean."

She nodded. "Lyle," she said a little more loudly. "Tell me about yourself."

The dwarf gave her a look over his shoulder. He seemed quite respectful of her, even if he wasn't particularly respectful to Justin.

"What d'ye want to know?"

"You said you left your home to come adventuring," she said lightly. "That's interesting, isn't it? And you're fighting at my son's side, so I was already interested."

"Ah, he's not so bad with a sword as we say," he said gruffly. "And me…well, there's not much to tell. I decided to find my own way rather than stay in the fortress. I haven't had as many adventures as I thought there'd be, but yer son seems to attract them."

Mary smiled at that. "Do you have any brothers or sisters?"

"One o' each. Twins. Older'n me. They were hell and never went anywhere apart. 'Course, they also couldn't stand each other. That was fun. Last I heard, they couldn't decide whether to train as blacksmiths or goldsmiths. Now, me ma was a stonemason, see, and she…"

They continued to walk as Lyle rambled about his family. To Mary's surprise, the story had the little touches she wouldn't have expected from a game. She looked at Justin and he smiled at her.

When she tilted her head curiously, he said quietly, "You

wondered what I loved about games? This was part of it—all these stories."

She had never considered that. When at last Lyle began to wind down and the corridor finally showed the faint promise of sunlight, she called, "Your turn, Zaara."

"I have nothing as interesting as Lyle's story, ma'am." The girl seemed almost shy. "Or yours, I'm sure. I'm only a mayor's daughter."

Justin snorted. "Merely your average mayor's daughter. She taught herself daggers and magic and ran away to kill an evil wizard. Normal stuff."

"Justin!" Zaara flushed. "I barely know magic, especially compared to your mother."

"She's—" He looked at Mary and she saw his mouth twitch madly. "Yes, I suppose she does know magic. Mom, why don't you tell them your story?"

"Now, now," she said, "if I tell all the details, where would my aura of mystery be? I prefer to be mysterious." She smiled at Zaara and Lyle. "But it's clear I could wish for no better companions for you, Justin." She stopped him and squeezed his hands. "It was good to see you. I'll go now." She hugged him. "You're doing well. We think of you every day."

"I think of you, too," he said. "Tell Dad I said hi."

"I will."

She continued to watch him as the world dissolved around her into darkness. Moments later, she stared at the entire PIVOT team.

"Is something wrong?"

"Well, someone called the cops on us," Nick said, "because a woman screamed bloody murder. So, rest assured, Mrs. Williams, the next time we put you in the game, there will be no spiders."

Justin watched as his mother's form faded before he rejoined his friends with a sigh.

"I never learned any of her spells," Zaara said mournfully. "Justin, she's wonderful. Imagine having a sorceress for a mother. You never told us that."

"I never knew," he said philosophically. When the other two gave him a confused look, he cleared his throat. "Ah…I mean, I never knew until…oh, whatever. Maybe the next time she's here, she can teach you some spells."

"I'd like that," she said.

He stared at where the sunlight slanted into the mouth of the tunnel—werewolf-free, so far—and considered their options. "So, what on earth do we do next?"

"Well…" Lyle sounded contemplative. He held up a crystal vial of something that sparkled like stars and blood and death all at once. Looking at it too hard made the young man's head ache. "We could use this potion I stole from the werewolves and kill us a witch. What do you say?"

CHAPTER SEVENTEEN

Jacob looked at the clock. They had eight hours and three minutes left—or, in more commonly accepted terms, it was 2:17 AM. He hadn't slept since four hours before the FDA had arrived the previous day, and he was fairly sure none of the others had either.

It wasn't that he hadn't tried. He had attempted to snatch a catnap a few times. He knew their chances of getting out of this hinged on their ability to think clearly, and that ability would go down the tubes increasingly the longer they stayed awake.

But nothing, not even pure exhaustion, could rob him of the sheer rage that circled through his brain. He was furious, he was afraid of spending the rest of his life in jail, and he was even angrier that this was what was dangled in front of him to force him to back down.

He hadn't done anything wrong.

Not that the FDA cared. The agents worked with the absolute certainty that their bosses were doing the right thing. As far as they knew, he was running uncleared experiments on a comatose patient.

With his head buried in his hands, and gave a groan that turned into a shout of frustration. "What the fuck do we do?"

When he looked up, Amber was seated in her chair and stared at the ceiling.

"We could back down," she said. "It's the first time. There's enough evidence to show we saw it would be safe and we could almost certainly get you off without jail time. I trust Jamie when he says that."

The lawyer had, to his credit, given them all their options. He was sure the man would prefer it if they backed down.

Amber, however, was a surprise—and one that made his blood pressure climb even higher.

"You want us to back down?" he asked her. "You sat through sixteen hours of brainstorming and you didn't say that. And you watched me come back from getting bail, you told Mary you'd keep fighting, and you told me you thought we were doing the right thing and now, you tell me we should back down?"

She said nothing and watched him with dark, inscrutable eyes.

"Let me tell you something." He stabbed his finger on the kitchenette table. "We did the right thing. We used technology with a good track record to give Justin a better chance to survive this. We're only in this mess because some assholes at big companies don't want their quarterly reports to take a hit, and I'll be damned if I let them get away with that. We will not back down."

"Really?" Amber said. "Because Nick and I have given you..." She looked at a sheet of paper. "Seventeen different ideas and you've shot every one of them down because the FDA might come down too hard on us. If that's what you're afraid of, you need to back down. If not..." She stood, braced her hands on the table, and met his gaze. "Then get over it. This is the last time I'm asking. Do you want to back down? You're the one facing jail time and I gave you my word fourteen hours ago that if you wanted to call this off, I'd back you. Nick said the same. Give us an answer."

Jacob stared at her. "No," he said finally. "Fuck them. I won't back down."

"Then the time for trying to stay away from downsides is over," she stated. "We have two objectives. The first is to keep Justin on this course of treatment without interruption, and the second is to make this treatment available to more people. Keeping the FDA from getting mad at us in the short term is not one of the objectives."

The two partners locked gazes until he nodded.

"Now," she said as if the prior confrontation had not occurred, "we do have an option. None of us will be particularly happy, but we do have it. We approach one of COMPANY X's competitors and give them a deal. We leak what's been going on with Justin, that the treatment got blacklisted by an FDA official who took a cushy position at COMPANY X, and we let their competitor swoop in and buy the rights to the treatment. They go to bat at the FDA and their lawyers take the heat. We'll probably be blacklisted but the treatment will survive."

Jacob and Nick—who had remained silent thus far—looked at each other. Jacob could tell the thought was as much of a gut punch to the other man as it was to him but one look showed that Amber wasn't taking it well, either.

"We said that we got into this to help people," she told them. "I don't know about you, but for me? It partly meant that I wanted to be known as someone who helped people. I don't want to have my reputation smeared, but if it's a choice between that and this treatment not getting out…I think the choice is clear."

He rubbed his face to try to move past the feeling that he couldn't think anymore, having been awake too long.

The phone rang and everyone at the table jumped. He shook his head and pushed it to Amber, who sighed before she answered.

"Hello? Hello, Senator."

The two men now straightened.

"One moment," she said. "I'll put you on speakerphone…there. It's only the three of us here. Your wife is grocery shopping and DuBois went to take a shower.'

"About time," Nick said and shuddered.

"I'm glad I caught you alone," Tad told them. "We don't have much time left, so here's the deal. Our mystery donor is Anna Price of Diatek Industries. She has offered to fund the project and smooth out any FDA wrinkles by folding PIVOT into Diatek."

The three of them fell silent.

"I assume from your silence that either the call has dropped or you feel much the same way I did," he said. "It's too good to be true, so there must be a catch, right?"

"Right." Amber's face said she knew what the catch would be.

"I've had my aides dig up every damned thing I can about Anna Price and Diatek," he said. "Much of their work is sealed, unfortunately, as it's for the Department of Defense. But with that said, she told me one story that I have fact-checked and found to be completely honest. When she and her husband were postgrads, their daughter was involved in a car accident, became comatose, and had to be taken off life support because they ran out of money. She started Diatek soon after, allegedly to make sure no other family had to go through that. A few years later, her husband killed himself. His death certificate officially says unknown causes, but we've dug up obituaries and news coverage from the time that make it very clear it was known to be a suicide and it was about Mina's death."

Jacob felt the hair stand up on his arms. All three of them stared at the phone on the table, unable to look away.

"We've found paper trails that, as far as we can tell—and we're not engineers or doctors but we'll send you what we can— suggest she's being honest about where Diatek's profits go," Tad continued. "She never took it public, so she has no shareholders to answer to, and that means many details can fly under the radar. However, she doesn't have any extra properties we can find, she doesn't have massive investment accounts, and her C-suite team doesn't seem to live the high life either. And…I don't know if I have to say this, but Department of Defense contracts are lucrative. The woman should have money."

A long pause followed before Amber blew a breath out.

"PIVOT isn't my company," the senator said finally, "so this isn't my choice."

"No, but Justin's care is." Jacob found a reserve of energy he hadn't been able to access on his own account. "What is your opinion, sir?"

Tad took his time before he answered. "I want him to stay on this program," he said finally. "I know I'm not a doctor, but I can't see how only sleeping with no brain engagement would be better for him than this. Mary tells me he's not only recovering, but he's also actually…growing up. He's making moral choices. Would I rather have him in a hospital bed, sleeping for months? No. But I don't know how to get there. Whatever other ideas you have, I'll let you think about them. Call me when you've done that."

"Yes, sir." Jacob ended the call and looked around at the other two. "So, what now?"

"Hmm?" DuBois entered the room. He smelled much better but his hair somehow looked exponentially worse.

Jacob decided to chalk that up to his sleep deprivation. He outlined Diatek's offer quickly for the doctor, who took a seat and laced his hands over his stomach. He seemed deep in thought, not yet inclined to speak.

"I'm not sure we want to do this," Nick said finally. He held a hand up to stave off argument from either of his partners. "No, listen to me. A private company that comes out of nowhere to get a ton of Department of Defense contracts?" He held his phone screen out. "Their first contract came within two years, and it was a big one. That's absurd. They've basically been bankrolled by the military and intelligence ever since, and it isn't even clear what they're paid to do. Which…well, we know what that means."

"We think we know what that means," Jacob said. "The military is also working on stuff like regrowing limbs so it's not like everything they do is bad." He sighed. "Okay, yes, it's probably bad."

"Either she's lying about the research on comatose patients or she's telling the truth, and I don't think we'll do a better job of researching that than his aides did," Amber said. "I say we start there. If we think she's lying, there's zero reason to trust her and we say no. That's only my opinion. If we think she's telling the truth, we have a judgment call to make, right? Because then, it's a greater-good kind of thing, and I'll be honest, I never liked those thought experiments."

"Neither did I." Jacob groaned again. "On the other hand, this is exactly what you were advising we do, only now, we don't have to persuade anyone. The deal is already made." He shook his head. "But I don't want to answer to someone I've never met. I need to know this won't be shut down and buried."

"If we don't work with Diatek, it will be shut down and buried," DuBois pointed out. "We can keep moving the lab but they'll keep finding us, and I don't think any of us have deep enough pockets to fight the legal battle indefinitely."

Down the hall, the door opened and the quick, light sound of Mary's footsteps followed. When she arrived in the kitchenette, she studied their expressions with laser focus. "I wondered why you were so quiet," she said. "Trouble?"

"Less than before," Amber told her. With a stab of humor, she added, "Although that's a low bar. Do you want my chair?"

"No. Sit." The woman looked at them expectantly until they explained Tad's offer.

"What do you think?" Nick asked her. "I think he wants us to choose."

"I think he does," she said slowly after a moment. "He's right that PIVOT is your company. He and I can't choose for you. But I will say that although Tad is maybe too quick to fall on his sword when it comes to his conscience, he doesn't like to force other people into bad decisions. What I've worried about for the past day is that he would sell out to the lobbyists to make this problem go away, but that's something he would never ask anyone else to do." She sighed. "I guess what I'm saying is that if he thought this was a real deal with the devil, he would either have rejected it outright or he would have made it himself rather than put it on your conscience. Him putting the ball in your court is his way to show that he thinks it's a good deal."

A surprised silence followed.

"Really?" Jacob asked finally.

"He…thinks we should team up with someone who's helping black ops?" Nick asked skeptically.

Mary raised her shoulders. "Apparently, yes. Whoever this woman is, he believes her story."

Everyone looked at Jacob. "Oh, I have to make the final call?"

"You're the CEO," Amber said, "and you're the one out on bail right now. I'd say yes."

He thought for a moment, then shook his head. "Nope. One moment." He wandered into the other room, tore up a piece of paper, and scribbled some instructions. "All of you, color in one of these bubbles. I won't look to see who does what, and I'll cast my vote in there."

They shrugged and he left them with the tiny makeshift ballots and went into the other room to think. Justin's pod hummed in the corner and the lights flickered on the side. The monitor showed that he was in a conversation with his two party members.

Jacob remembered Mary's expression when she came out of the pod the day before—oddly calm and confident. He remembered the hints that she and Tad had been disappointed in their son. They weren't anymore. The senator was right. This treatment wasn't only giving Justin a chance to return to how he had been. It was giving him a chance to try being someone new.

It was important.

He returned to his team, picked the ballots up, and scrolled through them with a smile.

"It seems we're in agreement," he said. He picked the phone up, dialed, and waited until he heard Tad's voice on the other end of the line. "Senator. Yes. We've decided that we'd like to accept Diatek's offer. How do we proceed from here?"

CHAPTER EIGHTEEN

Lyle had stopped arguing by the time the group circled to the witch's hut, but his disapproval was clear. As far as Justin could tell, he didn't trust anyone who tried to hire killers, which gave him a wonderful mental image of the dwarf operating as the world's best and worst assassin—someone who would always get the job done, only to come back and kill his client as well.

He, however, still held out hope that one side of this argument would emerge as the reasonable one, and he'd secured promises from both his teammates not to attack the witch right off the bat.

The door to the hut still stood open as they approached, and he decided to go in first. He was the one who asked them not to attack, after all, so should take the most risk.

From the darkness, the witch surveyed them calmly. "Are the wolves dead?"

"Tell me more about what happened between you," Justin said. "It sounds like you fought over the ruins. I'm interested as to why."

She tilted her head to the side and folded her arms. "Are they dead, adventurer, or aren't they?"

"Some witch you are," Zaara said, "if you can't tell." She raised an eyebrow. The group had decided that, even if they went with his plan, it would be way too suspicious for all of them to behave nicely.

"I can tell the forest is not regenerating," the witch said, "and I can smell a potion on you that I know is meant for me. However, I also felt an extraordinarily strong bolt of death magic in the ruins, and the three of you smell of that as well. What am I to make of these facts?"

Justin had the urge to tell her the absolute truth. The death magic had come from a relatively untrained sorceress who had been imbued with her powers by an all-powerful god and let loose to kill a single larger spider.

He couldn't allow the conversation to be dragged sideways like that, but it would be worth it to see the witch's face.

"I could ask the same thing," he said. "I've heard three stories now, all different and all pointing fingers. I've heard the people in those ruins did nothing to anyone except take the ruins when you wanted them—and that they weren't even ruins two months ago. I've heard, from yet another of the wolves, that they were bandits who crossed you and stole something of yours, only to receive a disproportionate punishment. And I've heard from you that they're thieves and murderers whose very existence is causing the world to die, although you won't explain how they became werewolves in the first place. What I want to know is—"

"So you didn't kill them," she interrupted. "They're still there. Their presence still taints the forest. Their pack still hunts the villagers and their flocks. Not only that, but you also came back with the means to kill me."

She raised a hand as casually as if she might shoo them away, but what came from her fingertips was a bolt of lightning.

Justin swung his sword up in time and the bolt of magic ricocheted off the blade to punch through the ceiling with a sizzle. He stared at her and disappointment twisted in his chest.

"You couldn't answer a simple question," he said, thoroughly angry now. "You know, when you tell someone to commit mass murder, it's polite to tell them why."

That was the signal. On the word "polite," Zaara flicked the lid of the potion open and flung a few drops at their opponent. The woman gasped, curled her hand around her forearm where the liquid had splattered, and looked at Justin with venom in her eyes.

"Yeah," he said. "That's right. I ask questions. I don't come in with my weapons drawn. But I'm not stupid either. Go!"

His teammates swept into motion. Lyle charged and tackled the witch into the back wall and Zaara circled behind Justin using a nearby chair to vault into the air and descend on the witch from above. Two blades, one steel and one silver, slashed and their enemy screamed. She lashed out toward the young woman and ripped her belt pouch away.

Thankfully, Zaara didn't have the potion any longer.

Justin saw the decision form in her head, and he lunged, his blade out to catch the bolt of magic that arrowed directly toward his partner's chest. He had no idea what it was but he did know he didn't want it hitting any of them. When the witch crumpled in a daze, he realized it had been a stun spell of some kind.

Lyle flicked a few more drops of the potion on the woman before he threw the potion toward Justin and Zaara. Had the dwarf been the kind of person who hesitated before launching into battle, he might have been moved to pity by the sight of a lone woman swaying on the ground, defenseless.

Luckily, he wasn't one of those people. He delivered a strong kick and followed it up with a hammer strike on the witch's head.

"Ha!" he yelled. "You can't shoot firebolts if ye can't see straight, can ye?"

"The man has a point," Justin called to Zaara. He waited for Lyle to dodge before he sliced down with his sword.

The witch, however, had somehow managed to activate some

defenses. Where blunt force had partially powered through, Justin's blade was stopped by a weakly-flickering shield half an inch above the witch's head. She looked at him with a smile.

Fire burst from her hands where they were planted on the floor.

The house was barely standing as it was and this would bring it down within minutes. He swore and dodged a line of flames on the floor before he drove the pommel of his sword down on the witch's head. It didn't strike but the shield flickered and died, which was something.

Zaara danced in and one blade inflicted a long gash down the witch's back. As she slid out of range, a death bolt like the one his mother had thrown launched to follow her. He lunged and realized too late that he didn't need to worry about whether he stepped on the witch or not. He caught the spell with the tip of his sword and batted it away.

"Take that, worst batting average in little league!" His spare hand shook the vial over the woman's head and the potion made contact with an unmistakable hissing sound.

"Oh, that is gross!" Zaara yelled.

Justin stumbled toward a fiery wall but took time to find a place to plant his feet. He looked back to see the witch's form melt into something green, tentacled, and terrifying.

"Oh, good," he said. "Medusa and Cthulhu had a baby. This is good."

"It can still be punched!" Lyle shouted triumphantly and delivered a kick as he raced past her and managed to land it squarely in her groin. When she doubled over, he punched her in the face.

"I didn't know that hurt for women." Justin slashed at a tentacle that snaked toward him and followed it up with several quick swipes as others tried to circle. "Jesus, do these things ever stop growing? Zaara, does it hurt when women get kicked in the groin or is that only a man?"

"It hurts when Lyle kicks you anywhere," she responded.

"Damned right it does," the dwarf agreed.

"Sure." He looked around. The smoke had begun to cloud the air and he could barely see the door. "Okay, last attack—all in."

"Are you sure?" she called.

"Very sure. Zaara first."

This had been part of the plan as well. The creature swayed on its feet and turned to look at her, but the woman had vanished out what was left of the doorway with Lyle at her heels.

By the time it looked for Justin, it was too late. It took the last of the potion full in the face and chest and a truly terrible scream ended in a gurgle when he ran it through with his sword. The monster's face flickered between forms as it collapsed, and he punched out a side wall without even looking for the door.

He wouldn't normally plunge his head into a swamp, but he did it this time without hesitation, bolstered by the memory that water couldn't carry magic. Then, sure that his head was not on fire, he stood with a groan.

"Okay, she—it…whatever—is dead. Very dead. Are you two…" His voice trailed off.

Zaara and Lyle stood together close by, their weapons still raised, and around them and the entire shack, a pack of were-wolves had gathered. The sun was setting and the moon was rising.

A full moon, he realized in horror.

"Shit," Justin said. Thoughts tumbled through his head. Maybe the wolves had used them to kill the witch or maybe they were as bad as she'd said. Whatever the case, there was another battle to fight and unlike the last one, they didn't exactly have a potion to make this one shake out in their favor.

To his surprise, the wolf that padded toward him lowered its nose before it transformed into a human. Around the circle, fur melted away and men and women exchanged glances with one another.

"You said she's dead," the bandit leader said to Justin. "Was that true?"

"Well, she's a puddle of goo," he said. "And it wasn't moving when I left. I'd say that counts as dead." His arms ached where he held the sword. "So, let's get this over with, then."

"If you want." The man held out an amulet on a gold chain. "Take this with our thanks. You will always have a safe haven here."

He stopped and squinted at the item. "Wait, what?"

The bandit leader did not smile. "I told you we could make a deal if you freed us, and you freed us."

"We also killed several of your band," he pointed out.

Lyle uttered a sound of disgust. "Ye're not good at bargaining, are ye, lad?"

The leader did smile at that. He met the dwarf's gaze before he focused on Justin again. "Yes, you did. But you also left one of them alive in the tower when you could easily have killed him. You escaped rather than unleash your necromancer on us. And, perhaps most importantly, we would have all been dead in the end if the curse had taken hold—all of us and the forest as well. That monster was an abomination and you have freed us."

Justin took the amulet hesitantly. It looked almost like a clock and each ray out from the center was marked with a series of cross-hatches he could not interpret. "What is this?"

"Do you see the way the middle shines?" At the very center of the amulet, a piece of gold seemed to catch the light in a strange way. "That means it's charged. Anyone who wears this and dies will be returned to the last place the amulet was charged, alive and unharmed. It takes its power from old magic, the nodes between the ley lines."

He raised his eyebrows and looked at it quizzically.

"One use per charge," the bandit leader said. "Use it wisely. If you appear in the middle of our temple, we'll help you, but it won't bring your friends and not all nodes are safe places." He whistled and gestured to his team. "Goodbye, strangers. I'll be interested to see what becomes of you."

When they were gone, Justin slipped the chain over his head. He looked at the other two. "And we still don't know the story," he said.

Zaara laughed. "You'd better get used to that," she said. "I have to say, though, your principle of only killing people who are already trying to kill you got us farther than I thought it would."

"Uh-huh." He knew better than to look at Lyle, who clearly still disapproved of the tactic. "So what now?"

CHAPTER NINETEEN

Mary put the last of the server cords into a large box and shook her head. Eight hours seemed to have vanished in the blink of an eye.

As soon as the PIVOT members agreed with Tad's proposal, logistics swung into motion. A fleet of trucks was being mobilized for the PIVOT equipment to bring it somewhere that was allegedly close but completely unspecified—and, she expected, classified.

While the rest of the team packed—undoing days' worth of careful setup in as little time as they could—Justin's game wound onward. There had been a battle of some kind, she gathered, but DuBois had glanced at the monitor a few times and didn't seem worried.

"I think…" Amber looked around. "I think that's it. None of the rest can be unplugged until we have the truck."

"Which was supposed to arrive an hour ago," Jacob said quietly. He shook his head. "Did we do a stupid thing?"

"No," she said stoutly. "Jamie said there was nothing too sneaky hiding in those papers…well, nothing along the lines of them hanging us out to dry. But there's a small chance Justin may now be classified as a banned weapon under the Geneva Convention."

"A small chance that what?" Mary asked.

"I didn't say anything," she said far too quickly.

"And I didn't hear anything," Nick said. Both gave her identical, pasted-on smiles.

Her quest for answers was interrupted by several men in suits. They strode into the room and stopped when they saw the smiles on everyone's faces.

"Why is this still running?" one of them asked and gestured to the pod.

"Ohhhh," Amber said. "You're not...I mean, you're from the FDA."

"Yes." He fixed her with a suspicious look. "It's been twenty-four hours. We're here to shut this down—and, apparently, take Mr. Zachary into custody again, given that shutting the experiment down was one of the conditions of his bail."

"Correction," the young woman replied calmly. She folded her arms and gave them a sweet smile. "It has been twenty-three hours and fifty-four minutes."

The agents stared at her and she returned it impassively.

"You'll make us sit here for six minutes?" the agent asked her finally.

"You could wait outside," she suggested. Her sweetness didn't waver.

The man stepped forward. "There is no way this will be taken down within the next few minutes. It wouldn't matter if it was six or thirty-six. You're done. All of you."

"And you don't have the right to shut it down until those six minutes are up," she reminded him. There was steel under the sweetness now. She gestured to the kitchenette. "So why don't you take a seat? We can make coffee if you'd like."

The older woman could only admire her resolve. Amber

wasn't a Southern girl, but she could certainly slay someone with kindness as if she were.

The agents looked at one another. They looked at their young adversary, who smiled insincerely. Their attention shifted to DuBois, now perched on a desk and munching popcorn, and Mary, who had changed into a suit and pearls. The lead agent pulled his phone out and strode away as he dialed. Whoever he called, he launched into a furious, whispered tirade in the kitchenette.

The other two agents remained in position and Amber pulled a chair out and sat.

None of them broke eye contact. It started as a contest to see who would back down first but it had gone on so long that looking away would only be more awkward. Mary settled her shoulders, stared fixedly at one of the agents, and tried to think what Tad would say when he had to bail her out of jail.

But where was he? She hadn't heard so much as a word from him since the call. Papers had been sent by courier, looked over by a harried lawyer, and signed. She had given her consent as Justin's guardian, and the papers had been taken away again.

That had signaled the start of a seemingly endless wait.

The lead agent's argument ended in the kitchen and he stormed into the room to stare at them, his arms folded. He did not, however, touch a single piece of equipment. No matter how pissed he was, they were right about his jurisdiction.

Mary finally looked at the clock. Two minutes remained and as she couldn't see the seconds counting down, a minute seemed like an eternity. When they were, at last, within the final minute, she let her head slump forward—only to jerk it up when she heard footsteps in the hallway.

The lead agent didn't seem to care. He stepped forward with a smile when Tad strode into the room with a blonde woman in an expensive suit.

"Thank you for your service, Agent Hyde," the woman said

smoothly. She held out a folder as the agent swung to face her in disbelief. "Your agency has been relieved of duty in this particular case. You'll find all of the details in here and your supervisor should call you—"

Hyde's pocket rang.

"Now," she finished. She handed the folder to him and moved to shake Mary's hand. "Mrs. Williams. I'm Anna Price." Quickly, she went around the room and correctly identified each of the people there—including, Mary noted, the two other FDA agents.

When Hyde returned from this particular call, he was white with fury. "Do you care to explain this?" he asked Price in a clipped tone.

She did not waste time in thought. "No," she said simply. "I must ask the three of you to vacate the premises, please. This project is now under the aegis of a different agency in partnership with Diatek Industries and is classified."

The man looked as though he couldn't believe his ears. "Classified?" He ground the word out.

"As such, given that you lack the clearance or project authorization, I must ask you to leave." Her voice held a warning now. She gestured to the door and waited.

"Who authorized this?" he snapped.

"That information is on a need to know basis," she told him. "And you do not need to know. Mr. Hyde, if you do not leave, I will be required to call law enforcement at this juncture. Should anything be lacking in the authorization paperwork—and nothing is—I encourage your supervisor to take it up with the Department of Justice."

Hyde knew when he was beaten, at least. He jerked his head at the other two agents and the three of them left. They strode rapidly down the corridor and slammed the outer door behind them.

"Excellent," Price said. She looked around the laboratory. "It looks like you've packed up almost everything. That's good. The truck will be along shortly to move Justin, and while it does have sufficient power to maintain the full operation of the pod, I would like you to keep the generator attached as a backup."

Jacob nodded.

She looked at all of them and smiled slightly. "Do you have questions?" she asked.

"Why are you helping us?" Nick asked immediately. Jacob gave him a furious look but he was intractable.

"I am not certain what Senator Williams told you about my personal life," she said. "Suffice it to say that I have first-hand experience with watching a loved one deal with traumatic brain injuries. Our understanding of what works and what does not is woefully incomplete, and much of the operating budget of Diatek each year is devoted to various areas under the umbrella of reha-bilitation, sleep cycles, and the activity of comatose brains."

"Is that what your company does for the Department of Defense?" Nick pressed.

"Nick." Jacob held his face in his hands.

"Your associate is right in the abstract," Price told him. "He would normally have a right to know who he is doing business with. Unfortunately, Mr. Ryan, I cannot give you specifics of Diatek's work with any other agencies. Those projects are classified."

Nick looked away.

"If you look carefully," the woman said, "you'll notice that your contracts specifically state that you will not be required to do any work on projects other than this one. I do not ask for your approval of my company. I have made choices you might make and ones you might not. On this much, however, we can be clear. Funding for PIVOT is secured as long as I believe you have not knowingly and recklessly strayed into territory that would be more dangerous to patients than currently-approved therapies. Are we clear?"

After a pause, Nick nodded.

"Any other questions? No?" She walked toward the pod. "Good, because I have several of my own. What did you use for the converters here?"

Mary watched the team walk away and turned to launch herself into Tad's arms. They held each other for a long time without speaking, neither needing any help to know what the other was thinking.

"I knew you would do it," she said. "I was afraid you would throw yourself under the bus sometimes, but I knew under the fear that you would do it."

"You know me far too well." He set her down. "And I take it you helped persuade them on this end?"

"I told them you wouldn't give them a deal with the devil," she explained. "Don't prove me wrong."

"I don't think I will—although I have to admit I empathize with Nick." He shook his head. "It's always worrisome when someone has such an ironclad moral code that includes shady things."

"Yes. Then again, you never know where help will come from." Mary raised her shoulders. "You're fighting for people like her to not have to make those choices, right?"

"Right." Tad put his arm around her while she rested her head on his shoulder.

"I want to see Tina," she said finally.

She surprised him with that. He looked at her, his blue eyes quizzical. "Tina...who Justin was on a date with? That Tina?"

"That Tina." She nodded. "Don't worry, I won't yell at her. She's...emailed me and wants to know how Justin is. I couldn't bring myself to reply but I think I need to."

"It would be good if she were to come here," DuBois said. He stood nearby and he gave them an apologetic smile when they looked at him. "I didn't mean to eavesdrop but I heard the name. I'd like to meet her."

"Why?" Tad asked him. He sounded deeply dubious.

The doctor cleared his throat and looked awkward now. "Well, ah…since you ask…Justin isn't responding quite how I'd like to having Mary in the game."

"I've hurt his progress?" She was horrified.

"No. No, I don't think so. I wouldn't have let you go in if you were hurting him."

"Why did you let me go in at all?"

"Well, it was a good idea in theory, and the first time produced a significant spike of brain activity that seems to have settled into a higher cognitive level." DuBois pointed at a graph, remembered neither of them could read it, and cleared his throat again. "I realized the second time that your presence was…it's difficult to quantify. Please understand that this is a sample size of only one patient and there are many factors in play."

"Yes." Tad had his senator smile on. "I completely understand your reservations, doctor, and we won't hold you to any guarantees so give us your hunch."

"My guess is that Mary's presence forces a false dichotomy on Justin's mind," DuBois explained. "Young adults go through a phase where they have the power to begin reshaping the world. They see it differently from their parents' generation and they, in many senses, operate in a world that does not yet exist, while their parents operate in a world that no longer exists."

Mary's brain hurt. She squinted and tried to make sense of what he'd told them.

"Under normal circumstances, this would not create any kind of break with reality," the doctor continued. "Social turmoil, of course, if both generations were aligned enough with one another, but that's not at play here. My hunch, however, is that in this case, he now perceives this world as Mary's world—his parents' world—and the game as his world. Her dropping into it only serves to drive him into viewing it as a world where he can make a difference."

"Oh." She understood that, at least. "I didn't think of that."

"Again," he said carefully, "I would not have let you go in if I thought it was actively harmful. I think there's much to be said for encouraging his interactions with real minds instead of only the AI. That said, I would like to see his response to someone his age and especially, given the circumstances, I think Tina might be the right person for this."

She looked at Tad and they exchanged minuscule nods before they focused on the man.

"All right," she said.

"We'll have to clear it with Ms. Price, of course," the senator added. "But we've seen tremendous progress so far. If you tell us this is something Justin needs, we'll try to make it happen."

DuBois wandered off, probably to interrupt Price's conversation and ask immediately, and Tad looked at Mary.

"So, you went into the game again?" He sounded wistful. "I wish he hadn't said that about it being bad for Justin. I wanted to go in."

"No, you don't." She shuddered. "There are giant spiders. Like, the size of a small horse. Oh, it was terrible. It was good to see Justin, but…spiders."

He laughed. "I missed you," he said. "Also, please tell me there's video of you and the spiders. Did you scream?"

"I might have had law enforcement called," she said with great dignity.

Tad buried his face in his hands and his shoulders shook with mirth. "Oh, God. This, I have to see."

CHAPTER TWENTY

It should have been a miserable night. After all, Justin and the others had nothing to do while they waited for fire to consume the shack and reduce it to ashes. They were tired, they were injured, and a swamp wasn't a great area to try to sleep.

He wasn't sure what genius had come up with the idea of a virtual reality that included mosquitos, but he was increasingly determined that when he got out of there, he would kick some ass.

However, the mosquitos heralded a change that happened slowly over the course of the night and was more than visible by morning. The swamp and forest had begun to return to life. Green shoots of grass showed in the patches of dry, brown vegetation, buds pushed through on the various bushes, and birds building nests busily in the trees—which, he had to say, did not look quite so dead as they had the night before.

The area didn't smell quite as awful, either. There had been a stale smell before, somehow even worse than rot, and there was now a bright smell he could only describe as green.

The three of them awoke refreshed and each of them yawned and stretched. Lyle cooked sausages while Justin and Zaara wandered over to take a look at the ruins of the hut. While the remains were still surprisingly hot, the teammates were able to make some progress sifting through them with long sticks they had set to soak in water overnight.

"It smells all kinds of weird," she said.

"That's probably the goo," he told her.

"I can't wait to see that. I bet it's gross." She sounded intrigued. "I keep wondering what she was. I can't think of any myths that talk about something taking a human form that's green and covered in…what did you call them?"

"Tentacles."

"Right. I'd never even heard of tentacles before."

"Boy, would the Internet surprise you."

"Huh?"

"Nothing. I—you know what, forget I said anything." He turned the remains of a book. "It's a shame we didn't get her books out."

"I don't think so." she shook her head. "This place reeks of bad magic. You don't want to know how she did her spells."

"Didn't you want my mom to teach you death coils?" he asked her and moved a piece of what he assumed had been the table. He must be close to the witch's remains now.

"That's death magic, not bad magic."

"You'll have to explain the difference to me."

"You really don't know? Well, the clerics would say there's no difference." Zaara rolled her eyes. "But there is. Bad magic—no, let's start with death magic. Death magic simply kills things, right? It's like you made a sword but you made it out of death. You don't burn someone to death or stab them to death, you—"

"Death them to death?" he asked.

"Yeah, basically." She shrugged. "It's not bad any more than fire is bad. Death happens. It's all around us like magic. I suppose the only difference is that you couldn't use a death coil for anything else." She shrugged. "Still, it's a spell you throw like any other spell."

"Sure." Where was the damned body? Justin continued to shove pieces of wreckage out of the way.

"Bad magic isn't done with magic. If that makes sense."

"It really doesn't."

Zaara thought in silence for a moment. She dipped her hands in the water and pushed a piece of the wall off the pile. "Ha. If you move quickly enough, you don't get burned. Um…bad magic uses the life force of things to make a spell work. You can do it with anything, including a person or an animal."

"A plant?" he asked.

"I'm not sure. I guess so."

"Well…" He gestured broadly at the area around them.

"Oh." Zaara looked around. "Yes. Of course. That makes sense. You know, I wonder if she wasn't right when she said the were-wolves were draining the forest. If the curse had to be main-tained and the energy came from living things…yeah."

"What a charming woman." Justin scanned the mess around them. "Why do you say clerics don't see the difference between death magic and bad magic?"

"Because they both kill people." She shrugged. "To be fair, they would also say killing someone with a fireball is equally as bad. They don't think mages should be trained for wars and they don't think there should be wars at all. Or bandits. Or…you know, whatever. The problem is, that doesn't help when you're dealing with one."

"That's very true." Justin dropped his stick and sighed. "Okay, I cannot find this body. It should be here."

"If it were a puddle of goo…maybe not?" She scowled. "I guess I don't know."

"You didn't see this stuff. It was as gross as hell. It smelled—it smelled so bad. There's no way we wouldn't see a mark on some of the boards or something, or a…chunk of tentacle." He shuddered dramatically.

"What are you saying?" Zaara stared at him. "She was dead when you left, right?"

"I cut her in half and she collapsed into goo that caught fire." Justin waved his hands. "To me, that means dead."

"I…well, I can see why you'd think that." She nodded. "I probably would, too. But you're the person saying she was dead and saying her body should be here if she were, so I'm not quite sure what to do with those two pieces of information."

"Oh, this is a nightmare." He stared at the ruins. "If she's still alive, that is a very, very bad thing."

"Let's think about this logically." Zaara leaned on her stick. "The curse on the werewolves was released, so whatever happened to her, she wasn't able to maintain that."

"That's a good point."

"I know, right? Second point…I believe the key is right there near your foot." She pointed. "I don't think she'd have left that if she ran away."

He crouched, scrabbled in the ashes, and hissed when his hands tingled with the heat. After a moment, he picked the key up and juggled it between both hands. "Good. That's good. Any third point?"

"Yes. I think the sausages are ready." She set off, using her stick to balance herself as she leapt across patches of water.

Over breakfast, they relayed their findings to Lyle. The dwarf, mistrustful by nature, was inclined to believe that the witch was still alive.

"Ye can never trust a witch to be dead," he said gruffly.

Justin had also begun to suspect that most dwarves could be described as deeply pessimistic.

"What do we do, then?"

"We get the hell out of here," his friend retorted. "The ruins are crawling with wolf-bandits…or bandits that used t'be wolves, or—"

"The bandits formerly known as wolves," he said.

"Ye have an odd way of speakin', lad. I say we go to that stash of treasure we found when we were creepin' around and get it out of here before anyone else finds it. Keep the key and pretend we never saw this place."

"Hmmm." He considered the suggestion. While making their way back to the witch, the team had stumbled across a buried hoard of treasure, something he was sure they would never have found if it hadn't been for Lyle. They had covered it as well as they could and gone on, afraid the wolves might catch up if they didn't. Now, however, it might be worth returning for it. "Good enough. Shall we?"

The walk to the cache of treasure was slow. He wasn't worried that they would be killed by the bandits. At the same time, he was certain it would be fairly awkward if they were caught making off with a large number of artifacts when the last person who had opposed the bandits for these ruins was now—theoretically—dead.

Luckily, the little cart the blacksmith had made for Justin provided them with a template for makeshift sleds, and they set about excavating with enthusiasm.

"There aren't any stories about cursed artifacts in this world, are there?" he asked.

"Why, are there in yours?" Zaara raised an eyebrow. "And of course there are. Cursed rings, cursed amulets, all of that."

"You only thought to mention that after I put on the amulet from the bandit leader?" he demanded.

"Hey, you didn't think of it, either." She shrugged and struggled to secure a chest of coins closed with twigs, which didn't work well. Eventually, she gave up and ripped a few strips off the end of her cloak with a sigh. "What do you think these ruins were?"

"I don't know." He frowned. "The bandit said they weren't ruins until two months ago, but there was dust in some of the rooms and we didn't see furniture, and this doesn't look like it's been buried all that long."

"Coins, goblets, jewelry." Lyle shrugged. "Any rich person might hide this. It's odd that they took the furniture and not this, which is more valuable and more portable."

"I'm beginning to think you're right," he conceded. "This whole place has too many mysteries and not enough facts. I'm ready to be gone."

The dwarf nodded seriously.

They loaded what they could take onto the carts and sleds and returned to the road.

By the time they arrived, all three of them were in a very poor mood, not to mention sweaty and covered in mosquito bites. Justin had now achieved BUG CHOW level 3, which only vaguely helped his mood. He wondered if appreciating the AI's sense of humor was a sign of delirium and decided it probably was.

Things improved marginally on the road, but not by much. They had to travel slowly to avoid tipping any of the cargo off, and their backs soon began to ache with the strain. Once in a while, they would rotate sleds, but the way they sniped at each other about messing up the equipment had begun to take the fun out of everything.

"Mo' loot, mo' problems," Justin muttered to himself.

"Stop muttering!" Lyle snapped. "And get yer sword. I hear a cart."

"Oh, shit." He stood and panted. "Shit." He looked at the side of the road while his brain worked furiously. They should haul the treasure to the underbrush and hide it, but he couldn't see how to do that by the time the cart arrived. Besides, the thought of dragging it out afterward and setting off again was too much to bear. From the looks on the others' faces, they were thinking the same thing.

A mosquito stung him and he thought back, wistfully, to the time when the swamp was a magic wasteland full of wolves.

To their surprise, they recognized the cart's driver immediately.

"Ho, there!" the blacksmith said heartily. "I wondered if I'd find you here."

"Are you coming to trade?" Justin asked dubiously. The bandits probably needed a good blacksmith as they rebuilt, but he wasn't sure about the man's chances of being allowed to leave later.

"Nah." He drew the cart to a stop, swung down, and patted the draft horse's neck. "I got to East Newbrook and thought, 'Now, those adventurers helped me and they'll try to haul all that treasure back.' I stowed my gear and here I am."

"You're not worried they'll rob you?" Zaara asked.

"I'm the first master blacksmith to grace their town in four years," he said seriously. "The mayor would give me his house if I asked. In any case, I see I came none too early."

Justin was too tired to argue much, but he also studied the man suspiciously as they transferred the treasure. "This is an awfully big favor."

"When I was on the way here, I remembered how much I liked life on the road," their helper said contemplatively. "Nights alone by a fire with the open sky. A blacksmith can't usually stray far from his forge, and who knows the next time I'll have the time to leave East Newbrook. Plus…you could call it good business to forge a good relationship with wizard-slayers who might come through with plunder and stories. In every town I've served, I've made it a point to buy an ale for the adventurers whenever they come through and it's never steered me wrong yet." He smiled and hauled Lyle up next to him in the front seat. "You two, climb in the back and we'll set off."

"He's right," Zaara said when she and Justin were in the back and the cart started to turn. She gave a huge yawn. "My father always said the same about buying adventurers a beer. He said they were useful."

"He certainly made use of me, I guess." Justin yawned as well. Her sleepiness was contagious. "Stop yawning, dammit. Also, he never bought me a beer."

"How about…I buy you one…when we…" A snore finished her sentence. She had pillowed her head on her cloak and passed out entirely, her cheeks still flushed from the effort of lifting and loading the treasure.

His stomach did the weird sideways leap it always did where she was concerned but before he could be overly troubled by that, his eyes drifted shut and he fell asleep to the sounds of the dwarf and the blacksmith singing folk songs. His dreams were full of gold coins and foaming tankards as the cart wound its way through the now-living forests.

"That's it," Jacob said as he stepped into the offices again. "DuBois says it will probably take twenty minutes or so to get everything hooked up in the truck."

His partners nodded. They stood in the kitchenette of the office, and if Nick was reading Amber's expression correctly, she felt as shell-shocked as he did.

"Final walk-through?" she said finally. "We should make sure we don't forget anything important."

"Sure." He knew this was her way to cope with big changes. It had been helpful at least twice as often as it had been maddening, although the two sometimes overlapped. He, meanwhile, told too many jokes, and Jacob tried to manage everyone.

Who had ever decided to let three engineers run a company? It was madness.

It was clear that they had missed nothing in the big lab. With all the pods and servers removed and after a thorough vacuuming, the area looked oddly small. If it weren't for the glass walls that enclosed the pod area, he wouldn't have been able to remember what it looked like at all.

"I wish we'd been able to get all the tape marks off the walls," Amber said distractedly.

"The landlord said this will be turned into a restaurant." Jacob shrugged. "They'll probably gut the place." He hunched his shoulders. "No one will remember we were here, will they?"

"The people who heard Mary screaming will remember it," Nick pointed out.

The other man cracked a smile, as did Amber, but he could feel their sadness.

"Hey," he said, in a burst of inspiration. "Do you remember five years ago? We'd just had the idea for PIVOT. We were in my room—"

"We'd finished a pizza," she said. "I remember because I'd started lifting that week and I wanted to order four more and you kept telling me to order one at a time." She snickered.

"That was a lifechanging moment," Jacob said. "Not a night we had pizza. Focus on the big picture."

She laughed. "I'll tell you that the next time you're hungry. Or…I would if I wasn't afraid to die. You get hangry, man."

Nick watched them banter good-naturedly. He was glad they weren't a couple anymore. The bickering that was so easy between them as friends had acquired a bad edge to it while they were together. He'd been worried their friendship would be ruined, but they'd both gotten over the awkwardness quickly.

"Did you picture any of this that night?" he asked them when they had finished their whispered argument.

"Any of this?" Amber shook her head. "Not a single part. Hell, when we got this place, I was over the moon. I couldn't imagine having an office that wasn't in my living room. As for the rest of it…" She looked out toward the corridor and they could hear the beeps of the truck and the occasional shout. No one sounded panicked. The Diatek crew seemed to view all of this as a fascinating challenge rather than merely another boring job, which had set the PIVOT group at ease.

"I know I never pictured it," Jacob said with certainty. "I was sure we would do some good work, hit a roadblock somewhere, and all get office jobs."

"You never told us that," his friends said at the same time.

"I didn't want to be a downer."

Nick shook his head. "And now we're working for one of the main contractors with the Department of Defense."

"We also have salaries now," the other man reminded them, "and we're millionaires."

They shook their heads.

"That one still doesn't seem real," she said.

"Live in the Bay Area long enough and it won't be," Nick joked. "Plus, what's a millionaire around here? Nothing. Dime a dozen. We'd only be special if we were billionaires."

"Given that we still own forty-nine percent of the PIVOT shares, that might happen." Jacob shook his head in wonder. "What do you all think now? Do you think we'll pull it off?"

"I think if it's possible, we will," Amber said. "Before, tons of stuff could have gotten in our way. Now, the only thing we have to worry about is whether we can think hard enough to do it. Justin's results are groundbreaking in and of themselves, and we should have a much bigger suite of test subjects within a couple of years."

Nick whistled. "And then, before you know it, they'll be flying drones in some kind of Ender's-Game-for-Coma-Patients dystopia."

"Why are you always so negative?" The other man threw an elbow at him.

"I'm a realist," he said with dignity.

She snorted. "You're both pie-in-the-sky dreamers. I'm the realist here. And I'll tell you what, one of the first things we'll do is hire an accountant."

"Uh-huh," Jacob said. "And one of the next things is you firing the accountant because you can't stand giving up any of your work." His phone buzzed and he glanced at it. "They're all ready. Apparently, it was relatively simple. Wait a second, he's still typing…he wants to know if there'll be popcorn at the Diatek labs or if we should stop on the way."

Amber burst out laughing. "That man. Anna Price has no idea how much of her budget will go to popcorn, does she? And he'll weasel his way into getting that popcorn machine back, I know it."

"I'm sure he was the one who bought it from us on eBay," Nick said. "DrDPopcorn was the username, and it was created on the day we sold it."

"Jesus." Jacob rolled his eyes. "That man must give his financial advisor heart attacks."

"This may surprise you," she said as they left, "but not everyone has a financial advisor."

"What?"

"Oh, you sheltered little rich boy."

Nick waited until their voices drifted away, put his hands in his pockets, and looked around at the room. So much had happened there—their first whole prototype, the first test drive for each of them in the pods, and the marathon of late nights as they adapted the video game they had bought. There was no way to count how many boxes of takeout had been consumed there or how many pots of coffee.

He remembered that he'd always been excited to come to work, though. Even when the news coverage was snide about the cost of their product or when the initial sales numbers didn't come in as well as expected, he had come in every day excited about the work—and even more so now that they had found a use for it beyond entertainment.

"Hey, man." Jacob stuck his head into the kitchenette. "Is everything okay?"

"I'm saying goodbye." He grinned and flipped the lights off. "I don't want to be mushy, but…in case no one's said this to you yet, I think your grandmother would be proud of what you're doing right now."

His friend blinked a few times. His eyes were suspiciously bright but he didn't make any mention of it, so he also pretended he didn't see it.

"Thanks, man," Jacob said finally. His voice was a little rough. "That means a lot. I like to think you're right." He beckoned to Nick. "Come on. There's only one thing left. Once the pod is installed, we'll all go get some sleep."

CHAPTER TWENTY-ONE

With their treasure safely stowed in the cart and Lyle chatting amiably with the blacksmith, Justin's dreams were pleasant ones of soft beds and feasts. He'd had enough turkey legs to last him a lifetime in this world. Right now, what he wanted was mashed potatoes and some of his grandma's dinner rolls.

And mac and cheese. God, he'd kill for mac and cheese.

He wasn't sure quite when his dreams began to change but slowly, the feasts began to turn darker. The beds were prickly, the food tasted like ashes, and he looked around at skeletons seated in the chairs nearby.

The air was clammy when he woke with a start. While he'd been asleep, a heavy fog had rolled in. Zaara slept with one arm thrown over her eyes. She snored softly, and he leaned against the side of the cart with a sigh. They'd certainly seen enough terrifying things to warrant a few nightmares.

He stiffened when he saw something moving in the mist.

The hair on his arms stood up and he sat bolt upright. He peered into the fog behind the cart until his eyes ached, but the shadow didn't return.

Still, his instincts prickled alarmingly.

Quietly, he clambered onto the back of the cart so he sat directly behind Lyle and the blacksmith. They had stopped singing folk songs at some point and both of them looked at him warily when they heard him approach. He couldn't tell whether he felt better or worse to know that they were both spooked as well.

"Did the silence wake ye?" Lyle's voice was unusually subdued.

He shook his head. "Nightmares." He tried not to speak too loudly and turned his head quickly when he thought he saw something out of the corner of his eye. If there had been something, it was already gone.

Or it had been nothing and he was jumping at shadows.

Lyle dashed that hope a moment later. "There's somethin' out there," he said in a tight mutter. "It came with the fog."

Justin made a snap decision. "I'll wake Zaara."

The blacksmith and Lyle both nodded, and his heart sank. He climbed down as quietly as he could before he shook Zaara's shoulder. When she turned her head and started to wake, he picked her arm up and put a finger over his lips. Her eyes opened and she frowned when she saw him.

He motioned for her to sit and peer out the back of the cart. It took long enough for them to see anything that she looked at him curiously a couple of times, but finally, something black flicked through the fog. He could almost imagine it was a tail, something impossibly fast.

She pushed herself back with wide eyes. Her face had gone pale and when she looked at him, there was genuine fear in her eyes.

That, in turn, worried him. He hadn't even seen her afraid in Sephith's tower. Angry, yes. She was easily moved to anger and contempt for those who hurt others but she was rarely afraid. Tense and fearful, she looked at him, and then at Lyle, who nodded to her and showed her his fist. Whatever was coming, the dwarf was—as ever—ready to punch it.

Zaara drew both her daggers quietly, and he went to get his sword.

They all knew they were waiting, and Justin thought not knowing what they were waiting for was the worst part. He found out very quickly that he was wrong when the first beast broke through the fog in front of them.

He honestly could not have said what it was. At first glance, he swore he saw something like the witch. Arms waved like an octopus and lashed toward him. The creature blazed closer so fast that Justin and Zaara, perched on the back of the cart, tumbled into it with a clatter of gold coins. The horse screamed and dragged the conveyance in wild jerks, and the blacksmith gave a full-throated yell.

The beast hurtled overhead. It was long, possibly scaled, and perhaps as slimy as a slug. It was gone too quickly for Justin to tell—either what it was, or how it flew. He was left with the impression of fangs and a long tail, something he decidedly would not want to meet in a dark alley.

Or anywhere, for that matter.

On the bench, Lyle yelled something. The blacksmith was hunched over his arm but still tried to calm the horses.

"He's wounded," the dwarf called to Justin. "Drive the cart."

"I don't know how to drive a cart," he responded and tried to push panic aside. "Zaara?"

"I'll do it." She clambered up the side and onto the bench. He heard her sharp intake of breath and a sudden oath to several gods. "Lyle, get him in the back—oh, *shit.*"

"What?" Justin demanded. He scanned the road behind them for the giant snake-monster. "What is it?"

Lyle jumped into the cart behind him with a thud and a second, less graceful thud heralded the blacksmith joining him.

Justin looked back and froze when he saw what Zaara had been looking at.

Whatever the beast was, it had claws of some kind and they had inflicted a long gash in the blacksmith's arm—he must have put a hand up to shield his head, he thought. The gash, however, was far from the worst of it. The skin at the edges of the wound had turned a deep black, a dark liquid oozed from the cut to mix with the blood, and from the hissing sound and the blacksmith's bone-white face, the pain must be horrific.

He ran to help Lyle lever the man down, who hardly seemed to notice them. His breathing was shallow and a thin film of sweat covered his face.

"Zaara!" Justin called. "Get the horse running as fast as you can. We need to get him to town."

Her reply, however, was drowned out by another scream from the horse. Above them, the beast slithered through the fog, and the clouds parted in front of the cart. What stood there, all fangs and claws and dripping blood, looked like the army of hell. The creatures were far from human and barely close enough for their appearance to be utterly horrifying.

Zaara, thankfully, did not hesitate. She whistled sharply and yanked on the reins to guide the horse into a wide arc. The cart plunged off the edge of the road into the tall grass with a jostle that made the blacksmith hiss through his teeth and circled to try to get behind the creatures.

The horse, all things considered, seemed happy to flee. She did not crack the reins—indeed, she had to pull back on them to keep the animal from running wild. The cart jostled over the ruts and her entire focus was fixed on the horse and the bumpy landscape ahead.

She spared only a moment to say, "We're still closer to the bandits' hideout and we can't get through that army."

Justin responded with a curt nod. Behind him, the blacksmith gasped with pain while Lyle yelled something. It didn't take a genius to guess what. With his heart sinking, Justin turned and unsheathed his sword.

The army pursued them with preternatural speed. Whether on two legs or four, each of the creatures seemed to be made of thick tar, melting slightly at the edges as if formed out of a void and a wish that didn't quite hold together.

He could easily bet that he knew whose wish it was.

The first to reach them looked something like a cat. Giant whiskers trailed away from its face and an all-black maw opened in a snarl as it leapt onto the open back of the cart.

Without hesitation, he swung a heavy downward slash that passed cleanly through but left a dent in its head when the tar reformed.

"That is disgusting," he muttered. He took a half-step back as it lunged and pressed forward again, slashing and thrusting.

"Justin!" Zaara yelled. A knife thudded into the cart near his foot.

"Thanks, but I'd appreciate it if you didn't try to throw knives and drive at the same time."

"No!" she yelled, exasperated. "Say the spell to light it."

"Oh." He dove to retrieve the knife, delivered an awkward, one-handed swipe with his left hand, and yanked the weapon out of the floor. "Ignis!" Before the cat-creature could react, he drove the dagger forward into the place where an eye should be.

It went up in flames so fast that his sleeve caught fire. He swore and flailed his arm, only to be entirely doused by a jet of ice-cold water in the next moment.

"I can't look right now," Zaara called. "Did I put the fire out?"

"Yes." Justin shook his head and brushed away the water that dripped down his nose. "Boy, this isn't gonna be one for the history books, I tell ya. If they're vulnerable to fire, though…"

He threw his sword to the side, kept the flaming dagger in his right hand, and began to conjure fire in his left. The army had scattered as the flaming corpse tumbled off the back of the conveyance but had now begun to reform—and they were pissed.

"Lyle!" Justin nudged him with his foot. "Go drive the cart. We need Zaara throwing fireballs."

"Someone has to keep him from bleeding out," the dwarf shouted in response. His hands were pressed against a wad of blood-soaked cloth. On the floor, the blacksmith had passed out. His face was an unhealthy gray.

"There is no time," he snapped. "Brace it with something—a chest, whatever. I don't care. We need to get to the bandit hideout and we need to keep these things at bay."

Lyle hurried to obey. He wedged the blacksmith in the corner with impressive—and, frankly, worrying—strength and climbed up to switch places with Zaara.

She dropped down with fire brimming in her palms and threw her first firebolt a second later. He thought it had gone wide until he saw the faint red glow in the fog above and a flaming bird-creature tumbled out of the sky.

He shuddered and returned to his fireballs.

By now, he was sure these creatures were not sentient. Anything that could think would know better than to pursue two humans who lobbed fireballs with wild abandon. Even chickens, he thought, were smarter than that. The beasts didn't seem to care, however. They pushed closer and closer and threw themselves into the path of the fireballs in order to give one another cover. They moved in twos and threes and some swooped down to distract the two defenders long enough for others to clamber onto the cart.

They would die there. The realization chilled him to the bone despite the heat from the fireballs that seared his face. The amulet the bandit had given him lay heavily against his chest, a reminder that he would almost certainly come back

But Zaara wouldn't and Lyle wouldn't.

With a roar of fury, Justin stepped in front of her.

"Ignis!"

He didn't have a word for the spell he tried to do. In fact, he wasn't sure if it was a spell. Still, he yelled, he drew on his magic reserves, and he pictured what he wanted. Against all odds, his vision appeared in his hand.

The sword was made of pure flame and bigger even than a claymore.

His palm seared against the hilt but he swung it anyway and whipped it viciously with a whoop of glee. The fire was so light that he might as well be swinging air despite the sheer size of the blade.

"Get—the fuck—back!" he bellowed. "Or I swear to God, I will kill you, and find you, and bring you back, and kill you again. Painfully!"

In the back of the armored truck, several Diatek employees stared, wide-eyed, at the monitors.

"Um…" one of them said faintly.

"Hmm?" DuBois, who had snored quietly in one of the seats, straightened with a jerk. He peered at the monitors and nodded vaguely. "That's normal, don't worry," he said.

Unperturbed, he rested his head again and went back to sleep.

The cart clattered into the bandit hideout with Lyle screaming hellos at the top of his lungs and Justin yelling threats at the top of his. To everyone's surprise, the army practically flattened itself against thin air as soon as they were inside. Beasts melted into goo and re-formed, howled, and clawed at a barrier Justin could not see.

"What the hell?" Zaara panted.

"Don't question it," he responded. "Just...you know...give thanks."

Bandits rushed out of the buildings around them and the leader shoved them away to reach the front. At Justin's urgent wave, he hurried to the back of the cart and his eyes snapped together when he saw the blacksmith.

"We'll take him inside."

"Wait." He removed the amulet and laid it around the black-smith's neck. "He needs this more than I do."

"Why didn't I think of that?" Zaara asked rhetorically.

"Because we were throwing fireballs at monsters," he said. "It's the same reason I didn't."

"Right." She stood aside as the bandits lifted the blacksmith down and carried him inside.

"I'm sorry to impose," he told their leader. "We...had nowhere else to go."

"You chose well," he said bluntly. "Something is wrong out there, and it seems we're safe here. Why, I don't know—and I don't know how long it will hold. Come inside. We'll explain there."

CHAPTER TWENTY-TWO

The man led them to what looked like a half-finished throne room. A massive stone pedestal stood in front of two tall windows. Some of the panes had shattered and the glass had, with efficiency, simply been pushed against the back wall. A fire burned in the hearth and a large table, roughly made from scrap lumber, had been placed in the center of the room. Around this, an odd assortment of chairs and stools had been placed.

Their host led the three adventurers to the hearth. "Sit and eat while I explain." He saw them look toward the door and smiled grimly. "No one will touch the goods in your cart by my order. We may not have always been friends, but without you and yours, this group would still be cursed. They know that."

Justin settled and accepted a bowl of stew. He was surprised to see both Zaara and Lyle rummage through their packs and put something in the stew pot—a piece of meat and a potato. She gave him a meaningful look and he dug out an onion and a carrot, as well as a strip of dried meat. He felt foolish. Once he had seen the custom, it seemed intuitive enough, but he had almost blundered badly.

He had never been much of a one for etiquette—all the

gestures seemed meaningless and empty, merely a way to hide the truth about a situation. He had to say, however, that he had begun to appreciate social customs more since he had been in this game. When even former enemies shared food, there was something to be said for it. *We might not be friends, but we're all trying to make our way in the world. I'll give you what I have and you give me what you have.*

"So," the bandit leader said and leaned back in his chair. "The curse has been lifted. We know that to be true."

Justin paused, his spoon partway to his mouth. It didn't take a genius to see the but coming—which was good since he wasn't one. He was, however, a person who had fought a nightmare army on the way there.

"Something is...not right," the man continued. He shifted a little and stared at the flames. "What is coming back is still strong. The grass grows as it should and the sun shines. But...it is as if our nightmares grow as well. When the witch was here, her spells drained the life from the land. Now that she is gone, the land thrives but it seems some of her evil remains."

Zaara looked at Justin, and the bandit caught the look.

"What? What do you know?"

"Well, for one thing," she said delicately, "we *don't* know your name. I'm Zaara, of Riverbend. This is Lyle, of House Stout. And Justin, who comes from very far away indeed—and whose mother is a sorceress of no small power."

"And I'm Hildon," the man said. He smiled. "Apologies for the bad manners, Mistress Zaara. Events are unsettled here. Now, will you tell me what you two were looking so meaningful about?"

She nodded at Justin, who considered what—and how much —to tell him.

"I told you that the witch collapsed into a pile of goo, yes?"

"Yes," Hildon said drily. "I remember that being a particularly evocative way of phrasing it."

"The reason I said goo was that she wasn't, er…human…by the end of the fight. She was green. There were tentacles. I killed her—it—and there weren't any bones like you'd expect." He left out the part where the body had been gone when he went back to look but added, "If it wasn't human, can we expect all its power to go with it?"

"That isn't good." The man considered this but glanced at them. "Would you like more stew?"

Justin, luckily, had the good sense to know the answer to this. He patted his belly and shook his head. "My belly is full, thank you."

"That army seemed like it wasn't all…there," Zaara said thoughtfully. "I almost wonder if we saw the same creatures or if they were simply echoes of our personal nightmares."

Hildon raised his eyebrows but said nothing.

"What else do we know?" she asked. She looked at Justin.

"They were vulnerable to fire." He ticked points off on his fingers as he thought of them. "They are growing even as life comes back to the forest and marsh, and they have outpaced the original dead zone." He looked at their host. "And there was trouble here too, apparently."

"Creatures in the dark," Hildon said shortly. He nodded at Zaara. "As if from a nightmare like you said—and disappearing so quickly that no one could tell what they saw. They never came over the walls, which we realized soon enough. But we didn't notice them before some of our hunters and foragers went missing."

Justin was momentarily diverted by this. "Do you have people in your bandit crew whose job it is to simply find food?"

"Of course we do," he said. He looked at him as if he were crazy. "How else are we supposed to eat?"

For a moment, all he could do was stare. He had assumed that bandits stole food like they stole other things. He shook his head by way of apology. "So they don't come over the walls.

That's right. They didn't follow us past the gate, even the big one."

"And it's not your magic," Zaara concluded, looking at the bandit. "For a spell like that, you'd have to have quite a sorcerer in your band."

"If we were that strong, we'd have killed Sephith ourselves and taken his tower," Hildon said with a snort. "No, magic is a rare enough thing—and powerful, even when the wielder is inexperienced." He gave Justin a wry look.

"Just so you know, I'm leveling up his Sick Burn skill," the AI told him.

Justin sighed but the man's words sank in and he stood so quickly his chair tipped. He picked it up, not looking at it, and walked to the block of stone.

"Justin?" Lyle called. In a stage whisper, he added to the others, "The boy's not right in the head. Ye'll have to forgive him."

"Yeah, yeah." He could see the hexagonal shape now and his fingers brushed away the dust to reveal tiny grooves—as if a frame of some kind would sit on the block of stone. "These ruins appeared out of nowhere a few weeks ago, yes? And they were perfectly preserved, as if no one had been here and no one had ever found them, yes?"

"Yes," their host said. He stood and moved to join Justin with the rest of the group. "Why?"

He pointed to the stone. "What you said about taking Sephith's tower made me think. This block of stone would fit his throne awfully well. It was a machine and sucked people's souls out of them and stored the energy to give it to him. When he sat in the chair, it gave him their power."

"This was Sephith's," Zaara whispered. She looked around. "But we only killed him two weeks ago and they said this has been here for months."

"I don't understand all of it," he said and shook his head. "It would explain some parts of it, though. The strength of the barrier spells, for instance. It seems like they protect whoever owns the ruins."

"They do," the bandit said. "When the witch said we stole something of hers, she wasn't lying—well, not exactly. She laid claim to the ruins first, but she left one day for some reason. We snuck in to check the storerooms—and when we had our people in the throne room, she couldn't get in."

Justin began to laugh.

"What?" Hildon looked confused.

"I told ye," Lyle said. "He's not all there."

"No, it's…" He wiped at his eyes. "It's…oh, God, my stomach hurts. One second. Ow. Okay. It's only the mental image of…" He broke down in tears of laughter again. "Of us trying to sneak into the ruins at night and running into an invisible wall at high speed."

Even Zaara snickered at that mental image.

"Ah, yes." Their host looked intrigued. "We did bring you here ourselves, didn't we? Otherwise, I suppose you would never have gotten in."

"Ye could have simply holed up," Lyle said.

"And lived in a stone warren for the rest of our lives?"

"It worked fer the dwarves, dinnit?"

Justin sensed the conversation going off-track and steered it back. "This is good and bad. The spells are still holding enough to protect the people inside the ruins but the ones keeping it hidden have already fallen apart. I'm not sure that staying here is something we can count on to keep us safe."

The others nodded as one of the bandits came into the room and drew Hildon away to mutter something in a low tone. The bandit leader frowned and replied, and when the man was gone, he looked at Justin.

"Your friend needs more help than we can provide. We've slowed the spread of the infection but we can't stop it."

He closed his eyes. "It's stronger magic than anyone could be expected to heal." He felt terrible guilt now. The blacksmith had returned to help them, and this was the reward he'd received for his trouble. Then, a thought occurred to him. "The widow—the one we found the wedding ring for. If anyone could cure this—"

"She could." Zaara ran to her pack and rummaged in it. "Everyone, check what you have. She gave us potions. Some might be able to keep him alive until we get him to her."

"You want us to go out there again?" Lyle demanded. "Are ye mad?"

"The boy, as you call him, is right." Hildon clapped the dwarf on the shoulder. "This is no true refuge—it's a trap. The longer we wait here, the stronger our enemy gets and the weaker we become. A bandit learns to never stay in one place for too long."

"Ye'd never make a proper dwarf," he said grumpily.

"That's as may be, Master Stout. Now, if you will all excuse me, I will tell my people to make ready."

"Your people—you're coming with us?" Justin gaped in surprise.

"You barely made it here alive and the enemy will only have grown while we sat. Not only that, but we also need to leave as well." The man paused. "And, I admit, I'm interested to meet this widow you spoke of."

"She's ninety if she's a day," he said flatly.

"That's not why." Hildon pinned him with a glare. "Any healer who might heal something like this is an ally worth having. More than that, though, curses and hidden ruins tell me we need someone with a long memory. There's no telling what she might know." He nodded at all of them. "Get some sleep. We'll be on the road within an hour or two at most, and you were near-drained when you arrived. We'll need your fire magic when we're on the road again."

"Is there anyone you can leave?" Justin called as the bandit leader strode away. "If what's out there is the witch's power, I wouldn't like the idea of it having a hideout."

Hildon paused while he considered this. Finally, he nodded and continued to walk away.

"Well, if we're abandoning this place, I'm having more stew," Zaara said. "You all should, too."

"I'd kill for a proper mug of ale," Lyle said wistfully.

"Think of it this way. If we go to East Newbrook, we can get some ale." He was only joking and so he was amused to see his friend perk up at this.

"That's true. I hadn't thought of it like that."

Lyle shook his head at Zaara, who grinned and lowered her head to hide her laughter.

"Well, then," Justin said. "For ale and honor."

"Ha." The dwarf nudged him with an elbow. "Now there's an oath. We'll make a dwarf of you yet, lad."

CHAPTER TWENTY-THREE

The bandits made ready to leave with surprising efficiency. A few came in to get bowls of stew, talked in low voices amongst themselves, and nodded at the adventurers. Some—Justin guessed it was those who had been on guard duty—came to take naps. They slept on the floor with their heads propped on their packs as if they could sleep anywhere at any time.

It was decided that a contingent would stay behind to guard the throne room and keep some of the horses.

"It's a risk," Hildon said when he asked him about it, "but so is going. A few, like your dwarven friend, had no interest in making the journey. He can stay with them if he likes."

Justin looked at Lyle, who was helping to tie packs down in the back of a cart. He was tempted to refuse on behalf of the dwarf but he knew that was unfair. However much he believed it was the safest thing to leave, he could not volunteer him for that.

To his surprise, his teammate shook his head when he asked if he wanted to stay.

"I owe ye my freedom, remember?"

"Lyle." He was smiling. "You've fought at my side since then. I think we can consider ourselves beyond keeping debts."

The dwarf gave him a considering look. "An' here I was, thinking ye were a useless city boy when we met."

"I was a useless city boy when we met." He grinned at him.

SELF BURN, Level 2

"Aye, true enough." Lyle shook his head. "But, no. I've seen enough from the two o' ye—I'll be safer at your side than anywhere else." He cleared his throat and looked away, his cheeks unusually ruddy. "Er…I mean t'say, ye'd be helpless without me. I can't leave ye, not in good conscience."

"You're a good man," Justin told him. He tried to catch Zaara's glance but she was watching the dwarf with a certain softness in her eyes. Curious, he pushed through the crush to her and helped her to load packages onto a cart. "Are you surprised by our friend's softer side?"

She didn't answer for a while. Her cheeks flushed, she swallowed. When she spoke, her voice was a little unsteady. "No one's ever wanted to…I mean…no one's ever said anything like that about me. My father never believed in me at all, not that way, and the people of East Newbrook tolerated me, but none of them would risk anything to fight with me." She cleared her throat again, a surprisingly gruff harrumph.

"Do you think you'll ever go home?" he asked curiously. "Go back, I mean. To Riverbend."

She considered this but didn't have the chance to answer. The carts had barely been loaded a moment before but they were already in motion, and Hildon trotted up to them with another of his leaders.

"Mistress Zaara," he said. "You'll ride with me. Justin, you'll ride with Mira."

He raised his eyebrows.

"Why?" Zaara asked. He was pleased to see that she didn't seem exceedingly happy about the idea of riding with the man.

"We have archers with flaming arrows in each cart," the bandit said, "but there's no knowing where we'll need reinforcement.

Mira and I will keep the two of you mobile so you can help where you're needed."

She looked at him and gave a quick nod—and, before he could react properly, she crushed him close for a hug. "Be safe," she whispered fiercely in his ear before she moved away and swung up in front of Hildon.

Justin, tongue-tied and afraid he was blushing, only lowered his head. He did, however, get an unpleasant glance at Hildon's smile as the bandit leader galloped away with his head close to Zaara's.

In the next moment, however, he was glad enough that they were gone. He didn't have the faintest idea how to get into the saddle of Mira's horse, much less while she was already there, and in the end, she had to swing down and let him struggle to mount.

She, at least, said nothing about it despite her fiery red hair and forbidding expression, which might have suggested otherwise. Oddly, she seemed to have a way of moving that was disturbingly lazy for someone so well-armed. He had the impression that anyone trying to surprise her in a dark alley would have their ass handed to them, and she wouldn't even break a sweat.

"Hildon will keep your lady friend safe," she told him. She looked over her shoulder at him with a wry smile. "I mean he'll keep her alive, mind you, not keep her looking at you with those gooey eyes."

"She looks at me with gooey eyes?" He straightened a little.

Mira sighed. "Yes. But Hildon's a flirt and he's a damned good fighter. If you're trying to be impressive on this journey, you'll need all the luck you can get."

"Luck?" Justin was outraged. "I'll have you know I conjured a sword of pure fire on the way here. I—oh. You were trying to get under my skin, weren't you?"

"A little." She flashed him a smile. "I'll tell you a secret, though. The one I want to impress will be in the carts and they're not pleased to see me riding with you. So, we both have someone to impress, eh?"

He grinned. If someone had told him a day and a half ago that he'd joke and fight alongside the bandits, he would never have believed them, but this felt oddly natural. "Let's give them a show, then."

Mira laughed and spurred the horse to a gallop. "Get ready, adventurer. We have monsters to kill."

"What's going on?" One of the Diatek scientists looked up in concern as the pod was lowered to the ground.

Jacob looked at the monitor and snickered. "Ahhhh. You'll get used to seeing that."

"Yes, but what is it? It looks like…" The scientist frowned at the neural activity readouts. "Attraction."

"Mm-hmm." He grinned at him.

"But he's the only person in there." The man still looked confused.

"I tell you what." The young engineer clapped him on the shoulder. "I'll start you on a strict regimen ofvideo games. We'll get you through a few, then you can come back to me and tell me if you still don't understand."

"Video games? But—"

"Trust me." He smiled. It had been a while since he had explained this and he found himself both wryly amused and struck by how little many people understood of this world. "Games give you a chance to be who you want to be. Humans don't turn into unfeeling robots simply because a person is made of pixels and algorithms. They still care. They still throw themselves into danger and try to help." He gestured to the monitor. "That's part of why Justin's getting better. Because the game helps him to be human."

The creatures didn't attack immediately. The caravan plodded into the fog beyond the gates and for a long time, nothing stirred. The mist swirled around the carts as Justin and Mira rode up and down the line. They could not see the entire caravan at once, but the vapor was not so thick that they couldn't see the road beneath the horses' hooves. Strangely, the clopping seemed to echo somewhat.

No one sang to pass the time. The bowmen kept arrows nocked and their heads turned constantly.

Still, enough time passed without incident to wonder if they had all been mistaken and if the magical creatures had ever existed at all.

The attack, when it came, was sudden and devastating. Justin and Mira were near the head of the line when the leader of the army—the worm that had flown over the blacksmith's cart and wounded him so grievously—exploded out of the earth in front of the caravan.

Mira's horse had been trained to go through battles but it was not ready for this. It whinnied and reared as the two riders leaned forward with all their strength. He clung to the horse's neck with one arm and Mira's waist with the other, and she leaned close to croon in the horse's ear. When the animal settled onto all fours, the bandit didn't hesitate and spurred it to a gallop as she tossed a glance at him.

He gave her a nod and held his right hand out. The power warmed it and brought a sudden rush of satisfaction. The witch and her minions had thought to attack them, but the humans wouldn't back down without a fight. This fucking-worm-creature—his new name for the army leader—would get more than it bargained for.

His gaze focused on its head as it flailed and tossed. When it swung to focus on them, he locked eyes with it.

"As soon as I shoot, turn the horse," he told Mira, and he launched one of the biggest fireballs he had ever created.

The creature had opened its mouth, whether to spit poison or snap at them, he didn't know.

Either way, it ate a fireball.

Its head exploded into flames and it withdrew into the ground with startling speed. The earth closed over it again. Rubble was strewn across the road but otherwise, it might never have been there.

Mira wheeled the horse and they surveyed the line. As the fucking-worm-creature attacked, other monsters had rushed out of the mist. The bandit archers called orders to one another as they knelt on the packs of supplies and fired. They reached over their heads with precision, nocked their arrows, dipped them in fire, and sent them with deadly accuracy. Tar creatures went up in flames with shrieks and ran wild, spreading the blaze to their compatriots.

Farther down the line, the rumble and roar of the road exploding once more caught his attention. The screams of horses and humans came through eerily, but his heart unclenched when he saw the glow of fireballs arcing through the fog. Zaara was still alive and fighting.

"Perimeter sweep!" he called to Mira.

She nodded and urged her horse to a canter. Under the range of the archers, she and Justin targeted the stragglers. It wasn't long before they developed a system. He scanned ahead and behind and his fireballs eliminated the enemy that had edged close to the carts. Mira, meanwhile, drew a blade that glowed a dull red and focused on the beasts within arms' range.

It took an odd kind of courage to trust her help, but once he accepted that he could rely on her to watch his back, it released him to fight with a focus he had never had before. He felt a deep satisfaction whenever he was able to aim a fireball with partic-ular skill and more than once, he felled an animal that had decided to attack her. She slashed and hacked with a skill that wasn't so much elegant as brutally efficient.

The caravan, aided by Hildon's bellows, kept moving throughout. The donkeys and horses had had their ears plugged and their eyes bound with cloth, and it was barely enough to keep them moving. Their flanks were shivering and coated with sweat.

The mist cleared so gradually that he didn't realize it until someone yelled from the front of the caravan. Something in the cart-driver's tone was enough to make both Mira and Hildon race to the front of the line.

Justin gaped. The witch stood in their path but she was truly monstrous. She was so tall that her head was lost in the clouds. Tentacles writhed and lashed forward, only to vanish in the space of a blink.

"Where did she go?" Justin yelled to Mira over the sound of the wind.

"Where did who go?" she called back.

"The witch—didn't you see her? The monster as tall as Sephith's tower."

She gave him a curious look and a chill ran down his spine. Whatever it meant that he was the only one who could see it, he didn't like it.

They had more pressing issues to worry about, however. At the front of the line, the first driver attempted to guide his horse out of the way as a massive worm hissed and swung its head. The archers fired as quickly as they could, but it wasn't enough.

When the worm saw Justin, it unhinged its jaw and its mouth yawned into a black void.

"Eat fireball, shithead!" he bellowed and hurled a fireball.

"What he said!" Zaara screamed and followed suit.

"Stooooooooooooout!" came the call from the back of the line.

"Thanks for the support, buddy," Justin called over his shoulder. Another fireball had already formed in his hand and he threw it. "Zaara, aim for the eyes."

And then catch it off-balance. Luckily, she seemed to understand his plan. The two of them threw fireball after fireball at the eyes while flaming arrows crackled and whizzed overhead. Finally, with a nod to one another, the two teammates gave the last of their reserves for a massive explosion that streaked forward in a white-hot inferno.

The screaming seemed to go on forever. The worm thrashed and shrieked, its skin no longer scaled or slimy but instead, burning far too fast. He had barely enough time to regret his choice before the creature expelled its last breath and black poison spewed into the air and dissipated. It fell and crumbled to ash, and the rest of the creatures vanished into the mist.

Ahead, Justin saw the widow's cottage through a swirl of fog.

"There!" he called. "Go, go! There's the cottage."

CHAPTER TWENTY-FOUR

The door to the dwelling remained tightly closed as the caravan thundered closer. Justin tried to jump from Mira's horse and barely managed to keep his feet from getting tangled in the stirrups. He still savored the memory of Zaara's hug but he wasn't sure her admiration would last if she saw him fall face-first into a mud puddle.

Common sense said it was best not to risk it.

The bandits lifted the blacksmith down while Justin went to knock on the door. The blacksmith's chest barely rose and fell now. His skin looked so pale that he might have been carved from stone.

"Please," he whispered. "Please, please." He raised his voice. "We need help! Please, we need a healer. I'm Justin, one of those who brought you your wedding ring."

At that, there was the sound of footsteps and the door opened. The widow looked out, bright-eyed and inquisitive, and when she saw the blacksmith, she clicked her tongue.

"Come in, come in. Well, a few of you. Only so many can fit, even if I was of a mind to take a whole bandit horde into my house—and I'm not." She looked at them all and counted. "You, bandit leader."

"Yes?" Hildon said with surprising courtesy. "I am Hildon, ma'am. Well met."

"Yes, yes, well met. Tell your band to come inside the wall. There's some protection in it, at least. And you, come inside with the other three. Where's the dwarf? Ah, yes." She looked over her shoulder and continued the stream of chatter. "Yes, put him on the table. Gently, now, he's not a sack of beans."

Justin gestured to Zaara to head inside and she smiled as she passed him.

"I'm glad you're safe," she said softly.

"I'm glad you're safe," he told her. He blushed and looked back to where Hildon ushered his people into the yard. To the young man's amusement, all of them tried very hard not to step on the herb gardens.

Inside the hut, the widow waved them to the hearth. "Make yourselves tea. The leaves are in the blue jar and don't use anything else. I won't answer for the effects if you do."

Hildon began to measure tea leaves into a copper strainer and hung a heavy iron water pot over the hearth.

The widow worked quickly and sniffed at the blacksmith's wound. Her look of distaste was plain as she hurried across the room to her workbench. A complex bundle of herbs went into the mortar and pestle and she sniffed now and again to check the balance. Finally, she poured a few drops of oil in—something that made everyone else in the room sneeze and which gleamed like pure sunshine.

Back at the table, she unwrapped the bandage on the blacksmith's arm. Justin, who expected something horrifying, was not disappointed. The flesh, streaked through with black veins, looked like marble and blood began to flow again as soon as the pressure was released.

"Exactly as I thought." She spread the paste she'd mixed liberally over the wound and held her hand out to Justin. "Your sword —the one I gave you. I need it for a moment."

He handed it to her and gaped in surprise as she placed the blade flat against the wound. Something seemed to change in the air—an almost electrical charge like a thunderstorm—and the hair on his arms stood on end. The widow passed the sword to him and bound the wound tightly before she placed her hand on the injured man's brow.

Justin had thought she was checking for a fever, but he watched a flush return to the blacksmith's cheeks when her hand rested there.

Hildon lingered close to his shoulder. "This woman is no mere healer," he said quietly.

The young man shook his head. "I swear I didn't know. I thought she was only an old widow."

"Well, your instincts surely led you right," the bandit leader said, "even if your guesses did not." His smile was wry.

The widow looked at them and he had the feeling she had heard the exchange. "Now," she said briskly. "Everyone sit and tell me why there's a demon's army on my road."

A long pause followed while she waited expectantly.

"A demon?" Zaara asked finally. Her voice sounded very small.

The healer snorted. "Surely you've noticed those are no ordinary creatures—and the one who summoned them is equally unusual."

Zaara shook her head. "If there were a demon wandering around, we'd have known about it before."

"It hasn't been here long. No more than a couple of months, I would guess. I felt something pulling the magic away but I wasn't fool enough to go seek it out." The old woman poured them all earthenware cups of tea. "Drink up, it'll give you strength."

Justin drank and was not surprised to see a buff appear in the corner of the screen. "I hoped the witch was the demon instead of there being two evil things that are still hunting us."

She chortled at that. "I knew I liked you, young man. And, yes. That witch was never a human woman. I don't suppose you managed to see its true form."

"Green," Justin said. "Oozy. With tentacles."

"Really? Interesting. Very interesting. Well, that answers some questions." She sipped her tea thoughtfully. "I wonder where Sephith found one of those."

"Sephith?" Everyone else at the table spoke in unison.

"Do you know of anyone other than him strong enough to summon a demon?" she asked. "No, of course you don't."

"Wait." Justin narrowed his eyes. "So the ruins appeared about two months ago, they seem like they were Sephith's, and that's when the demon appeared as well and claimed them." It was so close to making sense but he couldn't truly say it did yet.

"Precisely." The widow went to one of the walls and waved a hand. What had been bare was suddenly full of bookshelves. She selected one with a deep red leather binding and pulled it down. When she placed it on the table, everyone drew back from the set of diagrams.

As Zaara would have said, they reeked of bad magic.

"It's a binding spell," the widow explained. "The demon's life force and magic are what power the binding—or the illusion. It's not an exceedingly useful one for most people. For one thing, it takes almost as much power to bind the demon as it does to do the rest of it, and it's riskier. For another, there's a chance that it will break free at any time—and there has to be containment when the binding is broken, even deliberately." She closed the book with a snap. "But Sephith was never exactly a cautious person. If you want my guess, it suited his purposes fine."

"How d'you mean?" Justin took another sip of tea. It really was good. He couldn't tell what it was made from but the buff helped him feel better than he had in days.

"It was flashy." Her tone dripped with derision. "And my guess is he reasoned that if someone broke it or the demon broke out…

well, he'd be gone, so what did it matter if it ransacked the countryside?"

"That son of a bitch," Zaara said. Her voice sounded hot and angry.

"You're not wrong." The widow replaced the book and sat again. "The ruins—again, this is a guess—were likely a hideout, an entire city he could run to if he needed one. Whether the spell decayed and he simply didn't notice, or he pulled the power from it for some other purpose, I can't say. Either would be like him. He was sloppy. Powerful but sloppy." Her tone was deeply bitter.

He sighed. "So, I didn't kill her, did I?"

"You knew you didn't kill her?" Hildon's tone was overly sweet.

"I...might have noticed there wasn't a body or anything." He hunched his shoulders. "She'd already turned into a pile of goo, though, and the curse was gone, so that could have gone either way."

"Hmph." The man didn't look pleased but the reasoning was good enough to forestall a fight.

"No," the widow said. "You didn't kill it. To kill a demon is a tricky thing. It's not impossible but it is difficult."

"Wait," Zaara interrupted. "I don't understand something. The witch made the werewolves, right? She made that curse? But then she told us to undo it because it was draining the forest. None of that made sense to me."

"She was a lyin' bitch," Lyle interjected.

"You can hardly expect something different from a demon," the healer said wryly. "Be that as it may, however, the girl has a point. There's a reason I gave Justin a silver sword—werewolves have been known in this area for generations. I don't know how the first came to be, and when I heard mention of large wolves behaving oddly, I thought perhaps they had returned. I was both right and wrong. The demon did make them. It wanted an army of monsters to do its bidding, you see. I can't exactly blame it for wanting revenge after what Sephith did to it."

"It tried to make werewolves but realized the curse took too much power," Justin said slowly. "That makes sense. She was trapped in a weakened form—it was enough to trap us when we went into the hut but not enough to fight the entire pack of werewolves."

"And to undo a spell takes an investment of power, much like making one in the first place," the widow agreed. "It needed someone to get rid of the problem. It probably didn't see you coming up with quite that solution, of course."

"How do we kill it?" Hildon asked bluntly. He didn't seem at all interested in the lore. "You said it wasn't impossible, so how do we do it?"

The widow gave him a smile. "Very, very carefully, of course."

CHAPTER TWENTY-FIVE

The Diatek labs were vastly more impressive than PIVOT's had been. Amber wanted to be dispirited by that. She'd been so proud to be able to rent a space of their own and now, it looked shabby by comparison.

On the other hand, she wanted to drool at how many tools were laid out within eyesight. There would be no scraping projects together and McGuyvering solutions that might go wrong at a critical moment. They would have whatever they needed, whenever they needed it.

The pods were laid out in an orderly row. Nick worked with the Diatek engineers to get each of the unused pods hooked up while another followed them and made extensive notes.

She realized that Anna Price had come to stand beside her while she watched the activity. The CEO looked quietly pleased with the scene unfolding before her, but she could not forget the tone in her voice when the woman spoke of the trade-offs she had made to bring this company to profitability. She was very, very sure she did not want to get on the wrong side of her.

"Is there anything else you can think of that you need?" Price asked her.

"Nothing you need to bother yourself with," Amber said. "I know you must be very busy. We appreciate you taking the time to do this yourself."

"It's why I started the company." The woman glanced at her. "There's nothing more important. My C-suite knows that I am prone to disappearing at times. It's why I've been so careful in choosing them. Each is authorized to make decisions regarding their initiatives."

Amber looked curiously at her. "So there are other projects like this."

"There have been." Anna's jaw clenched slightly.

She knew better than to ask any more questions, and the pit of her stomach lurched. When this started, it had seemed so simple and it had seemed to work. She had to remember that there was still a great deal that could go wrong.

"I met a neurosurgeon once," Price said. She did not look at her companion and her gaze was still fixed on Justin's pod. "He specialized in a particular type of tumor that killed one hundred percent of the people who had it. Any lives he saved were considered a victory. I tell myself that we are in a similar situation with this work." She looked at Amber now and smiled. "Do not allow fear to blind you or the complexity of the situation to overwhelm you."

She nodded in response.

"I've made sure you have my number," Price said, in a way that suggested it was somehow already in everyone's phone. "Call if you need anything—at any hour. And..." She smiled again. "You know, I would like to try one of those pods if you don't mind. Another time, of course."

"Of course," Amber murmured. She watched her stride away and shivered for a reason she didn't quite understand.

Was this someone else's life? It felt like it.

The ritual the widow described was so complicated that Justin's eyes crossed within thirty seconds of her starting the explanation. Zaara, who he was beginning to think might be a terminal nerd where magic was concerned, leaned forward to listen but wound up staring at a single diagram with a shell-shocked expression.

"All of which is to say," the woman finished sometime later, "that I'll need to come with you."

Everyone had hunched slack-jawed in their chairs but now, they sat bolt upright with wide eyes.

"Wait, wait, wait," Justin protested. "We can't ask you to—"

"To what, child?" She raised an eyebrow. "Perform the spell only I know how to perform?"

"I have a question about that," Lyle said. He drummed his fingers on the table and frowned at the widow. "D'ye care to explain exactly how a widow in a tiny cottage knows all this about magic but never thought to stop Sephith?"

"Hey." Zaara looked up. "He's right. Why did you let him terrorize everyone? You hid away here, pretending to be a harmless old woman, but you could have helped."

"I couldn't, actually," she said. "I was the one person who would never be able to defeat Sephith." She looked at their confused expressions and sighed. With a snap of her fingers, she vanished and was replaced by a man who looked vaguely familiar.

Zaara's jaw hung open.

"You're the mercenary," Justin said. "The one who sent us into Kural's hideout and had us get the book."

"Ye bastard," Lyle added, for good measure.

The man smiled at him. "That book is how your friend first learned magic. I don't think you should complain, Master Stout."

"You're a mercenary who disguised himself as an old widow?" Justin asked.

Zaara made a kind of strangled noise.

"No," the man said patiently. "I'm a defeated wizard whose magic was chained by Sephith's spells. Once I finished wandering around like a heartsick fool after my defeat, I decided to see who I could train to defeat him. The world needed it, of course."

"You *are* Kural," Justin said, awestruck and faintly smug because his suspicions had been correct.

"Just so. And you've made quite an apt second pupil, might I say."

"Second?" Justin asked.

Kural looked at Zaara. "Hello again."

She gulped and finally regained the ability to speak. Her expression one of confusion, she looked at Justin and gestured to Kural as she shook her head. "This," she said, "is my magic tutor."

CHAPTER TWENTY-SIX

"Why didn't you tell me who you were?" Zaara demanded.

"Sephith bound my power but he wanted me dead." Kural stood. "He watched closely for anyone who could defeat him—remember how he told you he knew when people spoke against him? He did because he watched the whole of the valley. I did as much as I could for you in Riverbend, which he didn't watch as closely. There was less I could do for Justin." He gave the young man a sad smile. "More details will have to wait, I'm afraid. We need to prepare for the summoning."

Justin looked at the blacksmith who lay alone on the table.

"Watch." The wizard made a gesture and his spells became visible. They covered the wounded man like a blanket. "They will keep working, even if I am not here. What he needs more than anything is rest, however. Were I here, I would simply watch and wait."

He nodded but he felt a pang of regret mixed with fear. The man had promised to make him better armor but aside from that, he should never have been mortally wounded by demons.

Kural directed Hildon and Lyle to arrange potions and salves in three groups. The first would make weapons more deadly, the second would fortify fighters' strength or health, and the third would restore health. Every bandit was to have at least one potion, perhaps more.

Zaara and Justin, meanwhile, helped Kural prepare what was needed for the summoning.

"Summoning?" the young man asked.

"Yes—an angel instead of a demon. And before you protest, know that we will not truly summon it. It is merely to draw the demon to a place of our choosing. It will do anything it can to stop the summoning of an angel, of course."

"So we kill it while it's distracted."

"Exactly." The wizard pointed to two mortars and pestles. "Justin, grind the vervain. Zaara, you grind the thyme."

"Am I making a stew?" she asked under her breath but she set to work.

The two worked until both had aching arms and he realized his magic reserves had gone almost to zero. On a hunch, he twisted his arm with the pestle and the bar decreased slightly. When he examined both the bowl and the pestle, he noticed runes carved on them. It must be set to imbue the herbs with magic as it was used.

That explained why they had been in charge of grinding herbs, then.

Kural mixed a few herbs in careful proportions and stored others separately. Each packet was wrapped in a square of cloth that was slippery and silky, held together with a dollop of hot wax that glowed with spells. When he was finished, he gave his two assistants a critical look and retrieved two potions from one of his hidden shelves.

Justin had played a number of games where his character drank mana potions but he had never felt one take hold. It was as if he had swallowed an entire packet of pop rocks and washed it down with soda. His vision went blue at the edges as his mana bar climbed to full.

"Whoa."

"It is a good feeling, yes?" The wizard smiled. "There have been more than a few who got addicted. Be careful."

He nodded. "You have what you need for the summoning now, so what's the plan?"

"I'll need your help to devise one," Kural said bluntly. "I'll set a spell within a spell. The angel summoning will draw the demon close, then I'll release the second one. What I'll need, however, is someone to watch my back and people to keep the wider demon army at bay."

"Lyle, Zaara, and I can watch your back," Justin said. "The bandits know how to fight together, so it makes sense to have them fight as a group around us, and the three of us can alternate between more than one way of fighting when necessary." He looked at Zaara, who nodded, and then at the dwarf, who had recently entered the house. Lyle nodded as well.

"I don' have more'n one way of fighting," he said gruffly. "But when I punch somethin', it stays down."

"I believe you, Master Dwarf." Kural beckoned to him. "And I have something for you. This oil here will make your knuckle weapons deadly to anything of the demon realm. It is called Angel Fire, and it is quite precious. But, if ever there was a time to use it, that time is now, I think." He used another piece of the slippery cloth to smooth the oil over the knuckle weapons Lyle used and nodded at him. To Justin, he said, "I would appreciate it if you would convey the plan to our friends. I think someone they have fought with before would be a better voice to tell them what they must do."

He nodded agreement. "I will tell Hildon first," he said. "Any reservations he has may well show us a weakness in our plan. We will call you when it is time to tell the rest."

"Hey." Jacob beckoned to the technician he'd spoken to earlier. "Come watch this."

Not surprisingly, the rest of them crowded around as well. The essential work was done and they were merely bringing the excess pods online and updating now.

"This may show you part of why games are important," he explained. "When Justin first came into this game, his biggest goal was to get glory and win the...er, gratitude...of tavern wenches everywhere. Whatever you're thinking, it's probably worse than that. Trust me—I'll show you the logs. But watch what he's doing now. He's speaking to multiple people, asking them if there are problems in his plan, and then he'll speak to them about why they're doing what they're doing."

"But these...aren't people," one of the technicians said blankly.

"They behave like people and they look like people," he said. "Not only that but if Justin dies in the game, he may well die in real life. It's one of the ways the game works—it forces his brain into an acceptance of life and death." He settled into his chair. "Just watch."

Hildon listened to Justin's explanation with a furrowed brow. At his shoulder, Mira hovered with a carefully blank expression. When he finished, the two of them looked at one another. There was clearly some communication, although he could not tell what they had agreed. He suspected that was by design.

"You know what you're asking of us," the bandit leader said at last.

"I'm asking you to be the first line of defense against the demon army," Justin said. "It is dangerous and it will be difficult."

"And you're willing to admit as much to the bandits?" Hildon asked.

"Yes."

"Then do so." He gestured with his chin. "They'll pull no punches with their questions, I warn you."

Mira gave him a smile. "Good luck."

"I have to ask." He crossed his arms. "Do you expect me to do well at this or fail miserably?"

She considered the question. "I could see it going either way." With that not very reassuring assessment, she left to take her place among her comrades and Justin beckoned the others out of the hut.

He didn't want to share the entirety of the plan at a high volume in case the demon was listening, so he abridged that part and told them only about the fact that there would be a summoning for an angel.

Then he told them which people would do what.

"Hang on." One of the bandits, a woman with hair that was almost white, leaned against the wall and pierced him with a look. He was reminded of Lyle's assessment that old mercenaries had learned how to get other people to go into danger instead of going in themselves. It seemed it was probably the same with bandits. "We'll be slaughtered if we do this."

"Not slaughtered," he said. "If I thought you'd be slaughtered, I wouldn't have suggested this. There will be many waves of demons and it is imperative that whoever stands against them be strong and accustomed to fighting as a group."

"But you're putting us on the front line," another argued. Where the first was old, he was young, although his eyes didn't look any younger. "If we wanted to fight in the wars of the powerful, we'd have stayed in our villages. We don't get caught up in those messes."

"Do you remember what Hildon said at the ruins?" Justin challenged. "To avoid confrontation with an enemy like this is to let it gain strength."

"That was when we were trapped," the woman said.

"Now we can leave," the man agreed. "Who will the army

follow? They won't choose a group of bandits. They'll target the town."

"You'd let them attack the town?" he asked, horrified.

"They could be bandits too, 'cept they make themselves a target." The man shrugged. "Everyone makes their choice. If you have a house and flocks, someone will want those. If you stay in one place, you're a target."

He gaped and looked at Hildon, who seemed to be enjoying this. The man leaned against the wall of the cottage with his arms folded, and he shrugged.

"I told you they wouldn't be easy to persuade."

Justin thought about it. He did not look at Zaara or Kural and focused instead on the bandits. His father had once said that you could learn much about a person by really looking at them. At the time, of course, he had tried to convince his son to wear something other than jeans and hoodies, to which he had only rolled his eyes.

Now he thought he'd try to take the advice.

The bandits lived hard, but their gear didn't show it. Each patch was well made, and the gear was beautifully maintained. Leather armor and scabbards were oiled and worn easily. Knives were kept clean—cleaner than the bandits, in fact. These people lived and breathed defense, not comfort.

They weren't paladins, moved to protect the weak. Still, he suspected they weren't malicious, either. They merely tried to protect themselves and didn't see why other people wouldn't run as well.

In addition, they were used to being able to pick their battles.

"You came out here because you didn't want to live in their world," Justin said. The bandits had gone silent. They didn't nod but they no longer objected either. "And the odds were that you'd make it a few years before the world caught up with you. You knew there might be someone like Sephith or bored royal guards, or you knew that someday, you'd pick the wrong target or luck wouldn't go your way. That's how things go out here. Until then, you'd be free."

"Don't make a big deal out of it," a different bandit muttered at the same time that the AI popped up its input onscreen.

FLOWERY SPEECHES, Level 38

"Fine, I get it," Justin muttered under his breath. He shrugged. "You're used to being able to choose your fight. Well, this one wasn't what you thought. You chose it, way back when the demon was that one witch. You didn't even realize what you were stepping into. The thing is, now the demon is pissed and it's making an army and you have a choice—you deal with it now, or you deal with it later. You're looking at basically the only person around who can kill it, which means this is probably your best chance for a while, if not ever."

A sulky silence followed that.

"It sucks," he said. "I understand that. And if any one of you wants to switch places and guard the wizard while the demon tries to kill him, you're welcome to do that. It would probably be best if it's someone with magic if you have that. I'm doing this because the demon is attacking people I care about and I won't leave them. I think you all feel the same about those you fight with. In the end, though, it's your choice."

They began to talk and muttered among themselves. Tight knots formed. Some were arguing, he could see. Others had made their choice, and still more waited to see what others said.

They divided into two groups with two thirds on one side and one third on the other. It was clear what was happening, and he could only hope the larger group had chosen to help.

"We'll do it," Mira said, from the head of the larger group. She nodded at him. "You watched my back before, now I'll watch yours. Not to mention that I'd still be cursed if it weren't for you."

The two groups looked at Hildon now. Justin could see a certain fear in the smaller group. He didn't understand until the leader spoke.

"It's a heavy choice to make, isn't it?"

He realized then that those who didn't fight were relinquishing their right to be a part of the group. Horrified, he looked at Hildon,. "I didn't mean for this to happen."

"You didn't?" The man returned his look. "Where are you from that you'll keep someone with you even if they won't guard you through thick and thin? We don't guard townsfolk but we guard each other." He nodded at the smaller group. "I'm sad to see you go, all of you. I wouldn't have kept you in my team if you weren't worth it. May we never meet again."

"May we never meet again," the others murmured in response. They left, shouldered their packs, and vanished into the mist.

"Better to have fewer allies than uncertain ones," Kural said. "Shall we?"

"Yes." Justin swallowed and nodded. "There's a demon to kill."

"And a chance of killing it, thanks to you." Zaara squeezed his hand. "I didn't think you had a hope in hell of convincing them."

"Neither did I," Mira agreed.

"Thanks a lot, guys." He rolled his eyes.

"We weren't going to hamstring you by telling you that," Mira protested.

"Right. Let's go. And no one give me your opinions on our current odds, please." He shuddered. "I'd like to imagine a future where I survive."

CHAPTER TWENTY-SEVEN

Kural led the group through swirling fog. Justin couldn't see more than a foot or two ahead of himself, but the wizard seemed to know exactly where he was going.

Everyone else hung onto each other's cloaks to make sure no one got lost.

He was sure they would run into the same issue as the last time, with their enemy drawing out the suspense to breaking point and attacking en masse from the mist. Not so much as a flicker of movement caught his eye, however, and eventually, they stepped out of the fog with surprising suddenness.

Startled, he looked behind him. The mist hadn't met a wall, exactly, but it had ended within the space of a yard. It stretched up as high as he could see—which was unnerving, although he couldn't have said why.

"Come." Kural jerked his head at the group. "Down the hill. Quickly now."

They were in a piece of land that looked almost like a volcanic crater. It sloped down from sharp peaks on every side except for the small area they had walked in through, which seemed to have been worn down by the sheer number of people. The bare ground cut a path through grass of varying heights and ended at a patch of white ground—a rough panel of rock that might either be natural or somehow brought there long before.

It looked like the kind of place where druids might dance around naked, Justin thought.

Or the kind of place where someone would offer a blood sacrifice. He wondered if he should ask what exactly this ritual entailed but felt that it might be too awkward to do so now.

The wizard placed his packets of herbs on the ground next to the circle and began to work. First, he knelt and took a stick of charcoal out of a hidden pocket in his cloak. A giant diagram began to take shape on the white circle. It didn't look satanic, the young man thought. Not…exactly.

Only a little too close for comfort.

"Get ready," Kural said.

Justin, Zaara, and Lyle took their places around it and looked out. The mist had crept around the crater now.

It knew they were there. The hair on Justin's arms stood up and he gulped slightly.

The smell of herbs reached him. The wizard had cut some of the pouches open and followed the lines he had traced in charcoal as well as some he hadn't drawn at all. He didn't speak, but the sound of a muttered spell was almost audible in Justin's head.

The bandits were still fanning out when the first attack came. A set of bear-creatures lumbered out of the mist at high speed. They seemed to pull the vapor along with them as they ran.

Hildon's fighters didn't waver and flaming arrows were loosed immediately. Most struck home and all the bears met attacking bandits a moment later. Shouts erupted but so far, they seemed to be fighters calling to one another, not cries of alarm or pain.

Justin settled into a crouch. He held his sword angled and tried to breathe. Something out there in the mist was looking at him, he knew it.

It didn't come from where he expected. The ground directly ahead of him exploded and spiders poured out to skitter across grass and rock.

"Ignis!" he yelled. He shifted his sword to his left hand and swiped his right, the palm out, in an arc. Flames streaked from his palm and washed the spiders in a wave of crackling fire.

Some were obliterated but the problem with tons of spiders was that there were so many of them and they all moved in different directions.

"Spiders," he moaned. "Why did it have to be spiders?" He wasn't as afraid of them as his mother was, but that didn't mean he liked them. One of them had started to climb his cloak and he twisted and spun. "Dammit! Get off. Off!"

In the lab, Jacob looked around to see that everyone's shoulders were close to their ears. He couldn't judge, though, as his were, too.

"Hello, everyone," a cheerful voice said.

Under normal circumstances, an unexpected hello wouldn't have had much effect. However, as the technicians were watching the proliferation of demonic spiders on the screen, they were more jumpy than usual. Several uttered undignified noises that were outside their usual vocal range, two fell off their chairs, and Jacob almost took the monitors with him when he stood too quickly and promptly fell.

"Is everything okay?" Mary Williams asked. Beside her, Tad watched with an expression of deep consternation.

"It's fine," the young engineer said much too quickly. He shoved the monitor behind him. "Fine. Everything's fine here."

"How are you?" one of the technicians asked hastily.

"What's going on?" the senator asked and advanced on them.

He wasn't threatening, not exactly. But it was very clear from his expression that someone had better have a good answer.

"Let's say Justin could use Mary's help right about now," Nick said. He had recovered more quickly than the others. "She pulled out one of the most powerful spells I've ever seen in-game for a single spider, and there are about eighty-five of them right now."

"Eighty-five?" Mary asked. She had taken a step back but her hands had also come up in the spell-casting pose, clearly by instinct.

Tad looked at the technicians. He looked at his wife. Still utterly silent, he repeated the looks but with a deadpan expression.

"Is there, uh…" He cleared his throat. "Is there any video of that?"

***

"Get—the fuck—off me!" Justin yelled. He launched fireballs with wild abandon at this point, which seemed like a good idea until Kural yelled in protest. "Sorry!"

"I'll deal with the spiders," Lyle told him. "You deal with the big horse thing."

"What big horse—oh fuck, what is that?" He had the impression of hooves and bright red eyes and decided there was no time like the present for an offensive strike. "Geronimooooooo!"

The animal reared at the last minute and its hooves lashed out. He skidded to his knees and thrust the sword up with all his might. A red shield appeared at the point of impact. It glowed with demonic runes and the blade slid uselessly off it.

"Fuckballs," he said vehemently as he threw himself sideways. He barely managed to avoid rolling into the circle and the horse reared again. "How the hell do I—oh."

It was difficult to hold a visualization as he dodged around the animal, but he tried to imagine waves receding from a beach.

Oddly, that focus relaxed him. He began to dodge automatically, parried the stabs of the hooves, and jerked out of the way of its snapping teeth.

Waves…wave ebbing…waves—

He saw the entire shield illuminated on the creature, along with the places that held it together. Justin ducked under another reared attack, rolled away, and whipped to stab his sword directly into one of the glowing red runes.

The spell flared and a piece of it died.

"Aha!" he yelled. "What now, you piece of horsey shit?"

"I never imagined this as the backdrop of my greatest magical work," Kural commented in a long-suffering tone.

"It's better this way." Justin was on a roll now. He could see the points of strength across the animal's body and it couldn't keep all of them away from him at once. "Alone in a tower would be boring. This way, you have an audience."

"You aren't, of course, looking at me," the wizard pointed out.

"Oh, right. I saw that throne." He recalled Kural's hideout. "Look, I promise when this is over, we'll get you a parade and a ton of beautiful women singing new songs about how awesome you are, but right now—take that, you stupid horse—I need you to focus."

"Indeed," Kural said dryly. "I'll hold you to that, you know."

"I will sing both of you a song if you please shut up for a while," Zaara shouted.

"Killjoy." Justin dodged the horse's back feet and identified his opening. "Aha. One…two…three." A long slash of his sword cut along an unarmored part of the creature's side. Without the shield, the sword bit deep and he followed it with a fireball.

His adversary dropped with a scream.

"Oh, hell yeah. Giant worms? Demonic horses? Justin can do it all." He danced back and wished he could do jazz hands and hold a sword at the same time.

IMPRESSIVE KILLS, Level 1

"Level one?" he demanded of the AI.

"Do you want me to take it away? Because I can."

"Fine, fine." Justin looked around. Lyle was punching the last spider into the dirt, Zaara was surrounded by what looked like giant dead slugs, and the rest of the bandits seemed to be reforming their lines. "Is the first wave over?"

"It seems like it," Zaara said. "Kural, how are you doing?"

"Good. But I'm not quite where I need to be yet." He spared them a grin. "So let's hope there are a few more waves."

"Uh…" Justin looked over his shoulder. "I have bad news about that."

There was the sound of a particularly thick vat of liquid bubbling, and the demon strode out of the mist.

Everyone gaped at it and panic was evident on the faces of the bandits.

"Well…" Kural said. "Shit."

CHAPTER TWENTY-EIGHT

The demon strode forward with earthshaking strides. Each step was slow, but Justin assumed that it was merely for dramatic effect. They had a minute or two at the most unless it decided to make an evil speech.

"Kural," he said conversationally.

The wizard was gesturing to arrange the bandits in a peculiar pattern, although it wasn't clear why. It appeared to be a kind of a cone with an arc of bandits behind the circle as well. One hand still held the lines of power in the diagram, which now glowed white. He glanced at the young man. "Yes?"

"What kind of demon is this, exactly?" he asked him.

"Theoretically, it's a water demon." Kural cleared his throat. "Saltwater, specifically."

He looked at the green and faintly slimy skin. "So...fire magic?"

"Have you ever tried throwing a lit torch into the ocean?" He was pale now. "It would have about the same effect. The demon is stronger than I thought and my spell won't be able to kill it unless it's weakened."

"Oh. Uh...any ideas, then?"

223

"A big enough torch would do the trick," Zaara said decisively. "And you taught me that spells can be amplified, right?"

Kural looked quickly at her. "Yes."

"I can amplify Justin's magic and you keep the spell going. Help us when you can. We'll keep moving." She looked nervously at their adversary. "Hopefully, we can hold out."

"We can tell the archers to concentrate on one place," Justin said quickly. "Kural, where is it weakest?"

"The eyes," the wizard said at once.

"All archers!" he called. "Aim for the right eye! All melee fighters, concentrate on the left ankle. Focus on slowing it and direct your damage as much as you can to one area."

A yell of acknowledgment followed.

"The sooner we kill this," he shouted, "the sooner we can go have some ale!"

For that, he got a much louder cheer.

"You're learning," Hildon said from behind him.

"Thanks. Ready, Zaara?"

"Ready."

Justin tracked the demon's path. It led directly to Kural, whose face was pale.

"Hold out," he told the man. "Whatever it costs—this being won't accept a surrender."

"And I think I've used up my luck on near escapes." He nodded. "Do some damage. I'll spring the trap as soon as I can."

He caught Zaara's hand, ducked, and began to run behind one of the lines of bandits. She muttered under her breath as she started the spell to amplify his power and after a few moments, he began to feel the same tingly feeling as when Kural had given him the potion.

"Justin," she whispered.

"Yeah?"

"Start small," she told him. "You're not used to having this much power. Trust me. The first—"

The demon took its first step into the crater and the ground shook enough to throw everyone off their feet. Only Kural stayed standing and a white shield began to rise around him like motes of dust in shining sunlight.

"Archers!" Hildon yelled.

The bandits were well trained. The demon's giant head swung to find the source of the shout and the archers scrambled to their feet, aimed, and waited for it to stop. It had barely stilled when all of them let loose. The arrows found their targets, and although they extinguished quickly, it was enough to make the being rear back. One giant hand moved to its eye and it uttered a scream that Justin didn't hear in his ears so much as his mind. A series of red numbers floated up and away

"Melee!" It was Mira's voice this time. She raced forward with the melee fighters. Their group was ragtag but with their swords alight, they looked more formidable than they might usually. The demon looked down when their group reached its foot. Swords and spears swung in a flurry of blows before the fighters scrambled when the creature stooped to sweep one giant arm. A single bandit, the younger man who had challenged Justin, catapulted away with a yell and lay still.

Justin gathered his power and waited as the demon's head swung around. It looked at Mira, at Hildon, and finally, at Kural. When it stepped forward, the young man was ready. He gathered a small fireball in his hands—only enough to divert its attention—and lobbed it gently toward the right eye that was still steaming.

His plan, unfortunately, went awry. Instead of his intended restrained assault, a fireball the size of a small sheep singed his hair as it rocketed away. He stumbled, barely held his aim, and managed to hit the demon in the neck.

"And now you see why I said to start small," Zaara said.

"Oh, mama." He grinned. "Oh, I like this. Let's do that again."

"Let's run first!" She grasped his hand and yanked.

Mira's group attacked next to switch the order and keep the demon off-balance. They didn't shout war cries as they charged and simply ran. When the being swung to face them, they were already gone, having scattered behind it to circle. They had learned from the last time, Justin thought.

He loosed his next fireball at the same time that the archers shot and this time, they did enough damage that the creature's health bar took a noticeable hit. In a somewhat amusing twist, the health bar had been made a part of it, which meant that it was also obscured by the swirling mist and the demon's sheer height.

The next few assaults followed quickly. Emboldened, the archers began to fire without pause, and the demon could not find its footing to retaliate. Several of Mira's team collaborated to target the back of its heels, and although Justin suspected it didn't have an Achilles tendon, it bellowed in pain just the same.

"You're doing well," Kural called. "Keep at it."

That was all the demon needed to remember why it was there. Its mouth opened in a silent snarl as it looked at the wizard.

"Oh, shit," Justin and Zaara said at the same time.

The creature dropped its hand from its eye and stared at Kural. It took one step, then another. As if the fighters around it had only succeeded in annoying it, it turned and swept its arms forward and back. Tentacles that hadn't been there before lashed out and bandits careened away with a chorus of screams.

"Kural!" Zaara tried to run to him, only for Justin to yank her back. "Let me go."

"Don't get in its way," he snapped in response. Years of sword-fighting and months on the road had made her strong, and she was sneaky along with it. He had trouble holding on. "Listen to me. If Kural can't hold it off, what chance do you think you have?"

That made her hesitate—and the hesitation was enough. The demon surged toward the wizard at full speed. Justin, seeing

Kural as small as a mouse beside the demon, had one moment of deep regret before white magic exploded outward like a bursting bubble.

The demon skidded across the ground and lay still with its skin smoking. It was still moving, however.

He didn't want to warn it what was coming and merely raced forward and hoped the other fighters would see him and take note. Zaara caught up with him with enough time to pull his head down. His heart gave a sideway leap, but her words weren't quite what he had hoped for.

"I'll help Kural. Stay safe." She ducked away and left without giving him time to respond.

THIRD WHEEL, Level 1

"Now you're trolling me," he protested.

"Do you think that just started? Really?"

The demon pushed up and swatted at Justin, who skidded to a stop. It took another step toward Kural, who—he had to admit—did not look well. He was on his knees as he poured every ounce of energy into his summoning spell and his whole body shook. Around him, bandits lay prone and wounded.

And Zaara wasn't there to amplify fireballs anymore, which meant he had to get creative.

"Hey!" he called. "Hey, you. Yeah, I'm talking to you, fish-face."

The demon didn't spare him a glance.

"If I could give you negative levels for trash-talk, I would."

"Some demon you are," Justin called and ignored the AI. "You were summoned as a fucking contingency plan, you useless fucker. I bet your mom was a salmon and your father was a horny fisherman."

The demon swung to look at him. He couldn't tell if it was angry or merely bemused, but at least he had its attention now.

"You know what? You aren't even listed in the book of demons. When humans think of your kind, they think of bright red, flaming stone creatures, and now I know why. It's because you fucking suck. Where's your ingenuity? A proper demon doesn't do its own dirty work. It talks humans into doing it—but noooooo, you wanted to make an army of werewolves. How did that turn out?"

The demon began to flicker madly. One moment, it was gigantic and green, and in the next, it was the witch he and his team had encountered.

"Yeah," he said. "Yeah, you. Miss 'I need you to go fix the problem I made.' Great pitch. I guess I know why you didn't go into sales. Let me guess, Sephith found you in the discount demon bin, didn't he?"

<hr>

"Discount demon bin," Nick muttered. His lips twitched crazily.

Amber, who had snorted root beer up her nose, tried to recover without coughing soda all over the monitors.

"What's a discount demon bin?" DuBois asked.

"Never mind." Jacob patted his arm. "Have some popcorn."

<hr>

The demon stalked closer and its features shifted and writhed. "You are nothing, a useless human."

"Oh, yeah, sure, that's why you lost an eye and you're getting fucking owned by a horde of bandits and a level-three group of adventurers, huh? How's your eye, Cthulhu?"

Justin. It wasn't the AI, he realized, but Kural. *Lure it closer.*

"You wanna go?" He walked toward the being and spread his arms as he began to circle and drive it toward the summoning diagram. "Let's go. I'll even let you choose the weapons. You wanna—"

Someone pounded into him from the side. Justin went over

with a grunt of pain and hit his head so hard the whole world turned white.

Or…wait, the whole world had turned white. It wasn't the sickly gray of the demon's fog, either. It was a pure, blinding, light-filled white that illuminated the ground in lines that sizzled and burned and finally slammed closed around the demon.

It probably would have screamed if it had time, but it didn't. Where the lines fell across its skin, they seared through like a hot knife through butter. The creature didn't even go up in flames as there wasn't time for that.

Within seconds, it was ash.

Justin looked at Zaara, who had tackled him to the ground.

"Sorry," she said. "Kural said not to shout the plan where the demon could hear."

"A broken rib is…" He winced. "Probably better than death by demon. The jury is out, though."

"Let me help you up."

"I'd rather not move, thanks." He laughed, then regretted it. "Lyle?"

The dwarf appeared overhead. His knuckle weapons dripped with black blood and he had a psychotic kind of grin. "Let's find more demons."

"Oh, God." Justin closed his eyes. "Lyle Stout, demon hunter. It has a ring to it, I guess."

Around the crater, bandits struggled to their feet. Kural limped to those who were not moving. Hildon and Mira both tried to hold each other up and consequently didn't do a spectacular job.

Everything ceased when a loud, commanding voice asked, "What in the seven hells is going on here?"

He looked up to see the blacksmith. He was still pale but stood with his hands on his hips at the edge of the crater.

"Oh, hi," he blustered. "I'm glad to see you up and about."

"I woke up in a strange cottage in the middle of the mist and with what sounded like a full war going on," the man said. "And I think I remember a giant worm. And what's that?" He pointed at the diagram. "Did someone summon a demon?"

"Sephith." Justin took Zaara's hand and stood with a wince. "Don't worry, the demon's gone. Do you want to go back to East Newbrook?"

"Only if you promise there will be no demons," the blacksmith said. "I mean it. None."

CHAPTER TWENTY-NINE

Kural sent several of the uninjured bandits to retrieve supplies from his house and had others turn the battle-field into a makeshift hospital. Those who could still walk were tended to by Zaara and Justin once Hildon had taught them a basic spell to clean wounds.

The young man had never experienced the aftermath of a battle this way. Before this, he had simply stumbled to the nearest tavern and taken advantage of game mechanics to heal his tired muscles. Now, he had an up-close and personal look at the damage done by a battle.

Every so often, his gaze drifted to the edge of the battlefield where two bodies lay still. The young man who had challenged him—and been swayed, in the end, by his speech—had died in the demon's first attack. An older man lay beside him.

"It isn't your fault," Hildon said when he caught him looking.

He was making a splint for the bandit leader's twisted knee and wrapped the bandage as neatly as he could around the hard-ened leather of the man's scabbard. A short silence followed as he did not reply at first.

After all, he knew it wasn't his fault. He wasn't the demon and he wasn't the bandit. But still, he'd been part of how it had all played out.

"Every choice has downsides," he said finally. "I made my choice to try to persuade all of you and two of yours died for it. I know it would be worse if we had all cut and run. There would be hundreds of dead villagers and an army of monsters. That doesn't mean those two aren't still dead."

Hildon looked curiously at him. "Everyone dies. People die young, especially bandits and warriors. If you know such things are inevitable, why let them sadden you at all?"

"He's from a very different place than this land," Zaara said. She looked up from where she was binding a long cut on a bandit's side. "You should have seen him agonizing over what to do when the witch wanted us to kill you and you wanted us to kill the witch."

"Hey," he said, a little sensitive.

She bit her lip on any further words and moved to the next bandit.

"She doesn't think less of you, lad," Hildon said in a low voice. He smiled.

Justin's cheeks were hot. He finished the splint and looked around. There weren't many left to heal, and all of those were within Kural's purview, not his. He sat on the ground and rubbed his face as he realized he was exhausted.

"It can't happen," he said finally. Zaara wasn't real, and somewhere in a lab, a doctor watched all of this. He wanted to curl into a ball and die at the thought of people watching a romance between him and a fake character.

Thankfully, he didn't have to explain this to his companion. "A mayor's daughter and an adventurer?" the bandit asked thoughtfully. "I can see why you'd have your doubts."

He responded with a tight smile.

"Still," Hildon continued. "She wouldn't be the first well-born scion to run off and be an adventurer instead of marrying up. Mayors and merchants and the like always have plans for their children. And the children don't always like to go along with those plans, do they? It's somethin' to consider." He clapped him on the shoulder and allowed Mira to help him up. "Think about it."

Justin was saved from having to do this by Kural, who limped closer with Zaara and Lyle.

"Everyone is bandaged and healing," he said. "There aren't many serious injuries, I'm happy to say."

"Now to get back to the hideout," Hildon said. He sighed. "I'm not looking forward to a journey, I'll be honest."

"Perhaps you don't need one just yet." The wizard turned to survey the crater. He closed his eyes and bowed his head, his palms up.

The first change came with those who were gravely injured. Slowly, they elevated and thick sleeping pads appeared beneath them. An awning rose from nowhere to shelter them from the sun.

Beyond them, a creaking sound accompanied tables and chairs that sprang into being. A fire blazed into life on the white circle of rock with a whole hog on a spit. On the tables, platters of food appeared and their smell made Justin's mouth water helplessly. He could see pitchers of wine, bowls of roasted potatoes, and baskets of bread rolls. Two giant kegs of ale appeared at the edge of the crater, propped up on wooden stilts and accompanied by trays of mugs.

Kural opened his eyes and smiled. "Eat," he told those around him. "Rest. A journey should only be undertaken on a full stomach."

His suggestion was met with enthusiastic applause. Lyle appeared at the kegs with a speed that strongly suggested teleportation and began pouring ale for everyone. He appeared to have a process of drinking a mug of ale himself and pouring one for someone else, then repeated steps one and two as quickly as he could.

Justin laughed and sat. He was famished and he couldn't remember the last time anything had tasted as good as the pork and potatoes he shoveled into his mouth. He was on his third plate when he looked at Kural.

He watched the other man eating with perfect manners and asked, "Are you…I mean, is any of the three faces we've seen actually what you look like?"

The wizard glanced at him, surprised, and smiled. "You know, no one's ever thought to ask me that."

"I'll take that as a no," he said.

The man only smiled.

"So, what will you do next?" Justin asked.

Kural didn't answer immediately. He took another roll and offered him one as well, before—apparently on a whim—he conjured an opulent chocolate cake. "My biggest failure," he said finally, "wasn't in losing to Sephith. It was in leaving the people of the valley to his mercy—and mine. It was my spell, you know, that has ash floating in the air. I would like to undo as much damage as I can before anything else. There are buildings still standing at the tower and I can work from there." He looked at Justin. "What will you do?"

"I don't know," he said. "Well…I'll find the third key, I guess."

"I'll aid you if I can," the wizard offered. "I have several books that might contain some of the lore behind it. Sephith gave you my key and the demon…well, gods alone know where it found the one it gave you. I have my guesses but we'll likely never know. I'll send you a message if ever I find a hint."

"Thank you." They clinked glasses, a friendly and oddly reassuring gesture.

"And what will you do about your mayor's daughter, hmm?" Kural smiled slyly. "What will she do when she learns you're not of this world?"

Justin leaned back with a start.

"Yes, I do know." The wizard fixed him with a frank look. "It's obvious enough to anyone who has the eyes to see."

"Well, then, you make a suggestion." He met his gaze. "And she knows, anyway. She doesn't believe me, but she knows. And nothing will happen. I have to go back."

"Which is why you need the keys, eh?" Kural smiled. "We'll see."

The story continues with *Final Chance,* book three in the P.I.V.O.T. Lab Chronicles.

Coming soon to Amazon and to Kindle Unlimited

CONNECT WITH MICHAEL ANDERLE

Website: http://lmbpn.com

Email List: http://lmbpn.com/email/

Social Media:

https://www.facebook.com/LMBPNPublishing

https://twitter.com/MichaelAnderle

https://www.instagram.com/lmbpn_publishing/

https://www.bookbub.com/authors/michael-anderle

www.ingramcontent.com/pod-product-compliance
Lightning Source LLC
Chambersburg PA
CBHW070638100726
47907CB00007B/2029